MW01129117

More books in t
THE LOST TEMPLE OF TOTEC: BOOK ONE
THE ONE-EYED MULE SKINNER: BOOK TWO
THE BLACK PEARL TREASURE: BOOK THREE
THE HIDDEN FORTRESS: BOOK FOUR

ALSO BY ERIC T KNIGHT

IMMORTALITY AND CHAOS
(epic fantasy series)
Wreckers Gate: Book One
Landsend Plateau: Book Two
Guardians Watch: Book Three
Hunger's Reach: Book Four
Oblivion's Grasp: Book Five

CHAOS AND RETRIBUTION
(sequel to Immortality and Chaos)
Stone Bound: Book One
Sky Touched: Book Two
Sea Born: Book Three
Chaos Trapped: Book Four
Shadow Hunted: Book Five
Book Six – Winter 2018

THE ACTION THRILLER
WATCHING THE END OF THE WORLD

Follow me at:
ericTknight.com

All books available on
Amazon.com

ACE LONE WOLF
and the
One-Eyed Mule Skinner
by
Eric T Knight

ISBN-13: 978-1544917122
ISBN-10: 1544917120

Author's Note: The Lone Wolf Howls *series does not need to be read in order.*

1

As soon as the sun comes up, I'm going to be in real trouble.

Why? Because I'm lying on top of a giant anthill. Once the sun comes up, the ants are going to wake up, head outside and do whatever it is ants do all day. At that point, they're going to find me here and they're not going to be happy about it.

Lots of stinging will follow.

It's not the stinging that will kill me. No, it's the lying stretched out in the summer sun with no water. That's what will kill me. The stinging will just make it worse.

I pull on the ropes again, as hard as I can.

No good. The ropes don't give at all. The stakes they're tied to don't so much as wiggle. Those Yaqui bastards knew what they were doing.

How did I get here, staked to an anthill in the Mexican desert?

Well, there's this bloodthirsty Aztec god name of Xipe Totec. A couple companions and I found his lost temple and went inside and all kinds of crazy things happened, things I don't much like thinking about. It's enough to say that the adventure didn't end so well for me. On my way back north I was so busy feeling sorry for myself that I sort of forgot something real important. Like that I'm in enemy territory. I got down off Coyote to take a piss and four Yaqui Indians jumped me. I never really had a chance.

Lucky for me they weren't in a killing mood. More of a let's-torture-this-idiot-Apache mood. They staked me out on my back on top of this anthill. It's a big one. Home to thousands and thousands of ants. Red ants. The mean kind. The ones that are always in a stinging mood. I've tangled with red ants before and it wasn't what I'd call a pleasant experience.

What's still surprising to me is that after going to all the trouble of tying me up and staking me down, they didn't stick around for the fun. They took my pistols and my knife and rode off. Just a little while ago.

They also took my hat. One of them was wearing it when he left.

Somehow that bothers me most of all. I understand taking my weapons. I even understand the whole part about leaving me out here to die. The Yaquis and Apaches have bad blood that goes back a long ways.

But why take my hat? Yaquis don't wear hats. The only reason to do it is just to humiliate me more.

In case, you know, the whole being staked to an anthill thing isn't bad enough.

At least they didn't get my horse. They tried to, but Coyote's too smart. They never even got close. They didn't try that hard either, probably because Coyote doesn't look like much, being short-legged, long-jawed, and kind of a dirty yellow color. With crazy eyes.

If they'd gotten hold of him, they'd have been sorry, that's for sure. Because the other thing most folks notice right off about Coyote is he's mean. As mean as a snake with a toothache. He'd as soon bite you as look at you.

Like he knows I'm thinking about him, Coyote comes walking up.

"Hey, boy," I say.

His ears swivel toward me. He lowers his head and gives me a sniff. No doubt he's wondering why I'm lying here like this, when we have places to go.

"I could use some help," I tell him.

I can read the look he gives me. Coyote and I are close like that. The look says, You got yourself into this mess, you fool. You get yourself out.

"Useless horse. After all I've done for you."

Coyote wanders off and starts grazing. I'm going to have to come up with a plan that doesn't involve him.

How long can I survive here, stretched out in the sun, with no water? It's summer and hotter than the devil's frying pan, so maybe a day and a half if I'm lucky.

By which time I'll be nothing but one big ant bite.

I hear footsteps approaching and twist my head around, trying to see who it is. It's an old man, wearing a big, floppy sombrero and a tattered serape. He has a large bundle of sticks slung on his shoulder.

"Hey!" I yell. "Over here!"

He shuffles over to me. His feet are brown and wide-splayed in his huaraches. He has large, sad eyes. He looks me over. When he speaks, he has a thick accent, but his English is fairly good.

"Is not a good place to lie, Señor. There are many ants, and when the sun comes up…" He makes little pinching motions with his fingers.

At first I don't know what to say, his words are so unexpected. Does he not notice the ropes and the stakes? Is he blind maybe? But I can see his eyes and they don't look blind.

"Are you serious?" I ask him.

He nods sadly. "Is very serious. The ants, they will bite you many times."

"I know that. I don't *want* to be here." I tug at my bonds to show him I can't get away. The sun is very close to the horizon. It looks like a couple of early riser ants are already checking out this giant new food source lying on their doorstep. "You have to help me."

"I don't have any money, Señor. Nothing to rob. Only these sticks."

"Not *that* kind of help." Right then I get my first bite. It's inside my pant leg, up by my knee. How did it get clear up there without me feeling it? The bite hurts, and I want to thrash around and try to smash the ant, but that will be a mistake. If I hold still, they may go easy on me. If I go crazy, it's going to get a lot worse.

"You have ants in your pants, Señor," the old man observes.

I squint up at him. It's hard to see his face, shadowed under that sombrero. Is he playing with me?

"Do you have a knife? Can you cut me free?" Another bite, this one on my neck. This is not going to go well for me.

He ponders this, then slowly nods. "I do." He turns and starts to shuffle away.

"Wait! Don't leave! Cut me free first."

"The knife, it is not here. Is in mi casa."

"How far away is that?"

He shrugs. "Is not so far. I return by noon. Today, I think."

"Noon! That's too long!"

He turns back. "You don't want the knife?"

3

"I want you to free me."

He puts the sticks down, squats and studies my bonds. A couple more ants bite me. There's a lot of them on me now, crawling inside my clothes, across my face, exploring this strange new addition to their world. Trying to figure out if they should say the hell with it and simply sting it until it stops moving.

He fumbles at one of the knots. "I am old. I cannot untie this."

"Maybe there's another way," I say, desperately racking my brain for an idea. One comes to me. I whistle and Coyote comes trotting up.

"Get one of the rifles," I tell the old man. Both the Spencer and the Winchester are still in their scabbards, tied to my saddle. "Hold still," I tell Coyote. "Be nice and don't bite him."

The old man approaches Coyote slowly. Coyote lays his ears back and bares his teeth.

"Knock it off, Coyote! This is serious!"

I hold my breath as the old man moves closer. There's no way to know what Coyote will do. He doesn't like letting people other than me touch him, and he barely tolerates me touching him. His early memories of people aren't all that good.

Coyote makes this kind of threatening sound and his ears are flat to his head, but he plays nice and doesn't bite the old man or cave his ribcage in with a kick.

The old man draws out my Winchester and stands there looking at it.

"Is a very nice gun, Señor."

Oh, no. Is he going to steal my rifle and leave me here?

"I'll give it to you if you free me." I hate saying that. The Winchester is a nice rifle. I'd hate to lose it. But I think I'll hate being stung to a swollen lump even more.

He shuffles back over to me.

"Shoot the rope holding my hand." I notice that his hands are shaking quite a lot. Enough that I may get to add bleeding to death to the list of things going wrong with this day.

"It will ruin the rope, Señor. Is good rope."

"I don't care about the rope!" I realize I'm yelling at him and make an effort to get myself back under control. It's not easy. I'm collecting new ant bites at an alarming rate. I must have a couple dozen by now, but they're still just stinging me for fun. Any minute now they're going to get serious.

He points the rifle at my hand. "Do not move."

I *can't* move, I want to say. That's the problem!

But I don't. Instead I say, "Maybe you should get a little closer. So you don't miss."

The end of the barrel is about three feet from my hand, and it's weaving large circles in the air. Getting shot has gone from being a possibility to almost a sure thing.

"I do not miss," he says confidently, and squeezes the trigger.

2

Flame leaps from the end of the Winchester and the rifle bucks in the old man's hands. Something hot and painful stripes across my wrist.

I holler and jerk my hand back. Hold it up and count the fingers.

It's my lucky day. Only a little blood and I still have all five fingers. Looks like the bullet just scratched me.

But all that noise and thrashing around has gotten the ants all excited and now they're pouring out of their nest in earnest, waving their little jaws, searching for anything they can bite.

"Give me the rifle!"

The old man looks startled, but he gives it to me. I quickly shoot off the rope holding my other wrist, then the ones on both ankles.

I drop the gun and leap to my feet. I've got ants everywhere. I go into a crazy dance then, jumping around, slapping at my clothes, swearing.

In the end I have to strip off all my clothes. The ants are in every nook and cranny and it's the only way I can get them all.

Finally, the last one is gone. I stand there naked, taking in the damage. The venom courses through my veins like fire. I have big red bumps everywhere, arms, legs, torso, face. Some in places I don't want to mention.

I notice a strange wheezing sound and look up to see the old man bent over, his arms wrapped around himself. The strange wheezing sound is coming from him. Is he having a heart attack?

"Are you okay?"

"Sí, Señor," he replies, straightening and wiping his eyes. "Is very funny, the dance you do." He waves his arms and takes a couple dance steps. That starts a new round of wheeze-laughing and he has to stop and try to get his breath back.

"I don't see what's so funny," I grumble. "You wouldn't be laughing if it happened to you." I pick up my pants and pull them on.

He gets his breath back and straightens. "Sorry, Señor. To be this old, I have only the laughing. It is laughing that keeps La Muerte—death—away. She does not like the sound."

He probably has something there, but I'm not ready to laugh along just yet. I finish getting dressed and pick up the Winchester. He watches me. I look at the gun. I've never owned a rifle this good before. He's just an old man. There's nothing he can do to stop me. I see in his eyes that he realizes the same thing. Now he's waiting to see what I will do.

I hold out the Winchester to him. "Here. We had a deal."

He takes it, looks down the sights, whistles. "Is a fine gun." Then he gives it back.

"I have my chickens, my small garden. I don't need it. I think you do, a man whose enemies tie him to the anthill."

I'm not sure what to say. I stick out my hand. "Thank you. Without your help, well…"

He takes my hand softly, gives it a tiny squeeze, then lets go of it. "De nada." For nothing.

"If there's anything I can do for you?" I pick up his bundle of sticks. "I could carry this to your home."

"No. Is not so far. I don't have much to do, and is too early for my morning siesta."

I watch him shuffle away, wondering. How does he even survive out here, all alone and without a gun? I feel like there's a lesson here somewhere for me, but I can't figure out what it is right now. The pain from the ant bites is making it hard to think.

I whistle Coyote over and haul myself into the saddle. Then I sit there, not sure what to do next.

The obvious thing would be to go to Pa-Gotzin-Kay. That's the old Apache stronghold in northern Mexico where my clan lives. They've been there since my mother led them away while the U.S. Cavalry was moving my people, the Chiricahua Apaches, to a new reservation, after deciding to take back the reservation they'd already given us. Which was itself land they'd stolen from us. At Pa-Gotzin-Kay I'd find food and shelter. I'm sure they have at least one pistol they could spare me as well.

But I already know I'm not going to do that. Why? Because I feel like a dadgum idiot, that's why.

7

Dee-O-Det, the old shaman who is my clan's spiritual guide, told me not to go to the temple of Totec, and I did anyway. I don't want to listen to him say I told you so.

I also don't want to admit how badly I got played. I don't want anyone to know how that whole rigmarole played out. All that gold and I got none of it.

I point Coyote north and tap him with my boot heels. We'll go to Tombstone. I can replace my pistols there. Not sure how, since I don't have any money, but hopefully something will come to me.

Even when I have money it can be hard to buy guns, especially in the Arizona Territory when you look Apache. I'm not full blood. My father was a card sharp and small-time outlaw out of Texas and if I was to cut off my hair I could pass for a white man. At least part of the time. I've been told I'd have fewer problems if I cut my hair, but I'm not going to and that's that.

I haven't gone very far before I cut across the trail of the Yaqui braves that staked me to the anthill. The trail leads east. I sit there on Coyote looking down at it, and all at once I know what I'm going to do next.

I turn east. I'm going to get my hat back.

3

The Yaquis didn't make much effort to hide their trail. Probably they figured there was no chance I was getting loose and coming after them. They're going to regret that little bit of carelessness.

I find myself wondering something. Why go to all the trouble of staking someone to an anthill, and then not stay around to watch? It's not something I'd like to see, but if I was so inclined that way, and I'd gone to that much trouble, wouldn't I want to be there to see what came of it?

Not that I'm complaining or anything, but it doesn't make sense to me.

I follow the trail all day. I take my time and I'm careful, using my looking glass to check out the land in front of me before crossing open areas, staying off ridgelines and hugging cover wherever possible. I skirt any good ambush spots I come on, in case they've seen me and one of them doubled back to lay in wait.

It's almost sunset before I see them the first time. They're down in a low area and it looks like they're stopping for the night. From how many trees there are I'd say there's a spring there. I hear a gunshot and some birds fly up, then a couple more shots.

I ease up on them, nice and slow. There's a light breeze blowing from the east and I'm careful to stay downwind of them, so as not to alert their horses.

It must be a good spring. The land around it is thick with cottonwoods and willows, even a couple sycamores. There's a good deal of grass and lots of arrow weed. The cover will make it easier to sneak up on them, but also harder since there's more twigs and dead leaves to give me away.

Once they're asleep, I'll sneak in and get my hat and my guns back. On the way out I'll steal their horses. That will teach them to stake Ace Lone Wolf to an anthill.

I sit there as the sun drops and realize that this is actually the best I've felt since the temple. The truth is I've been moping, feeling sorry for myself. But lying on that anthill, thinking I was going to die, has helped clear things up. The self-pity is gone. I feel alive again. I guess almost dying has a way of clearing things up.

It gets dark and I hop down off Coyote. I reach into my saddlebags and pull out my moccasins, swap them out for my boots. Boots are great for riding. Not so good for sneaking around. I pat Coyote on the neck and he trots off to graze. I don't have to worry about him giving me away. He doesn't get along with other horses any better than he gets along with people.

I start making my way through the trees. Their fire's too small to see, but I can smell it. I go real slow, take one step, wait a few minutes, then the next. The whole secret to stalking is patience. Being in a hurry just gets you killed.

It takes better than an hour before I get close enough to see them. There's four of them sitting around a tiny fire, just a few twigs burning really. The horses are picketed a few feet away, grazing. The Yaquis are wearing a mix of traditional clothing—tanned leathers, moccasins, feathers—and white man garb.

One of them is wearing my hat.

Looking at it, I have to admit it's not much of a hat. It's black, but a faded, worn out black, and the crown has been smashed down so many times it's basically shapeless. The brim sags in some places and is torn in others. Really, it looks like something you'd take off a dead man.

I have a moment of doubt. Maybe this is a really bad idea. I could probably root around in the trash in Tombstone and find a nicer hat. Maybe I should get while the getting's good.

But those thoughts go away pretty fast. This is about more than the hat. This is about a man and his pride. I badly need a win, especially after what happened with Victoria and Block—I mean, Blake—back at the temple.

The man wearing my hat has some little bones tied in his long hair and a wicked lump on the side of his nose that makes me think it was badly broken in the past and never set right. He's shorter than me, older too, with lots of lines carved into his face by the years. There's a battered old rifle leaning against a rock next to him. Tucked into his belt is one of my pistols. The other one is sitting in his lap. From the way the other three defer to him, I'm guessing he's the leader.

Nothing to do now but wait. I ease myself into a bit more comfortable position, which doesn't help all that much, on account of all the ant bites I have.

But when I shift, one of the horses throws its head up and starts looking around.

I freeze, thinking the animal must have heard me. The four braves all sit up, and hands go to guns. I start to ease the hammer back on the Winchester.

Then I hear the hoofbeats and I settle back down. There's someone coming through the trees from the north. It sounds like two horses.

The Yaqui braves melt back into the trees, rifles in hand. One of them comes straight for me and for a moment I think he's going to step on me.

Instead he stops just to my right, up against a tree trunk. I could easily reach out and grab hold of his ankle if I wanted to. Thinking about it gives me a terrible urge to do it. I smile in the darkness, thinking how he'd react. He'd probably crap himself.

And then shoot me. Which wouldn't be so funny.

Lucky for me, his attention is focused across the campsite, not down by his feet. The hoofbeats get closer. There's a grunt and a low curse and my ears perk up. That sounded like English.

Then a man rides into the clearing and I can't believe what I'm seeing.

It's Ike Clanton.

4

The last time I saw Ike Clanton was after the gunfight at the OK Corral. He was studded with cactus thorns and headed to jail. Where I thought the good people of Tombstone would promptly hang him. Did he escape?

And what is he doing *here*?

Instead of shooting Ike on the spot, or maybe running out and stabbing him, the four Yaqui braves come out of hiding, lowering their guns. Which means they've been expecting him.

Ike climbs down out of the saddle and stretches. "Thought I'd never make it," he says. "It's a few more miles than you let on, and your directions were damned hard to follow."

He looks like he's recovered all right. Except for the ear that Morgan Earp shot off. That thing's not looking too good. It looks kind of like someone chewed up a potato and then stuck it to the side of his head. I wonder if he can still hear out of it.

"You bring guns?" the Yaqui leader says.

That's interesting. Ike Clanton is running guns to the Indians. Not that I'm opposed to such a thing on general principles—with proper weapons maybe my people could have held onto our land—but both the American and Mexican governments have pretty dim views of the practice. Ike better hope that Colonel Kosterlitzky and his Rurales don't get wind of him. If they catch him, he'll wish he was back in jail in Tombstone.

"Yeah, I brought 'em," Ike says, jerking his thumb at the mule he's leading. He takes off his hat and smacks it against his leg a couple of times to knock some of the dust off. I can see the bullet hole in the crown, so it's the same one he was wearing during the gunfight, the one I shot a hole in. "I got the whiskey you wanted, too. You got the gold, Yooko?"

Yooko nods. Ike goes over to the mule and unties a burlap-wrapped bundle, brings it over and drops it beside the fire. Yooko peels back the burlap and reveals about a dozen rifles. Yooko picks up one of the guns. The stock is in pieces and the metal is rusted. "This black powder," he growls.

"Only two of them are," Ike replies. "I told you it might happen. It's not as easy to buy a passel of rifles as you might think. Too many, too fast, and the law gets suspicious. Things get hot quick."

Yooko paws through the rest of the rifles and grunts. I can't tell if it's a satisfied grunt or not, but at least he doesn't shoot Ike on the spot, so that's something.

Next Ike unties a wooden crate from the mule's back. He brings it over and sets it by the fire. Pulling his knife from its sheath, he pries off the lid. Inside are a dozen bottles of whiskey packed in straw. He takes one out and hands it to Yooko. Yooko's grunt this time is decidedly more enthusiastic.

Yooko pulls the cork with his teeth and takes a long drink. He lowers the bottle in a fit of coughing and choking. No doubt it's the worst rotgut Ike could find. Maybe it's even kerosene. Maybe Ike's going to get shot after all.

But Yooko smiles big, nods, and passes it to one of the braves.

"The gold," Ike says. I notice he's got his pistol out, though he isn't pointing it at anybody yet. "This ain't a charity ride."

Yooko digs around in a rolled-up blanket, pulls out a leather pouch, and tosses it to him. Ike looks inside, pokes around a bit, pulls out a pinch of gold dust and lets it trickle back in. He closes his eyes, holds the pouch in one hand, and moves the hand up and down a few times.

He opens his eyes. "Feels light."

Yooko scowls. "No."

"And I say it is." Ike spits in the fire. "Y'all trying to hornswoggle me, is that it?"

"What is this 'hornswoggle'?" Yooko asks. "Not know this word."

"It means cheat. We agreed on eight ounces of gold. If this is eight ounces then I've got chicken gizzards for guts. Which I don't."

The Yaquis rattle off something between them. I don't know much of their language and only catch a few words. It sounds like they're deciding whether or not to kill him. That cheers me right up. Maybe they'll do me a favor and kill each other off. Be no problem to get my hat back then.

"Just so you fellers don't get any cute ideas," Ike says. "I brought a friend. Let 'em know you're here, Luke."

From back in the darkness comes a gunshot. The Yaquis break off and get really still.

"See?" Ike says.

Yooko smiles, showing his long, yellow canines. It's not a smile that makes me feel warm inside. It puts me in mind of a cougar brought to bay.

"A mistake. Only mistake." He reaches into his shirt pocket and brings out another pouch, which he tosses to Ike.

Ike tucks it away and gets all smiley in return. "There's no reason this can't be a friendly transaction." He puts his gun back in his holster and pats it. "Now that's over, we can have a real pleasant evening so long as everyone plays nice." He moves up closer to the fire.

"You boys got anything left to eat?" he asks. Yooko gestures and one of the braves picks up a quail carcass lying in the dirt. There's not much more than bits and scraps hanging off it. He tosses it to Ike, who eyeballs it.

"Can't see a damn thing in this light," he mutters. He looks down at the fire. "The hell kind of fire is this, anyway? Buncha damn savages." He picks up a couple sizable pieces of wood and tosses them on the fire. They flare up almost immediately. "That's better. Nothing like a good, civilized fire to make a body welcome."

He grunts and sits down next to the fire, brushes some dirt off the quail carcass, and starts gnawing on it. He looks up. "Pass that bottle over here now, and let me have some."

The brave holding the bottle looks at Yooko, who frowns a little, then shrugs. He hands the bottle to Ike, who takes a long drink and wipes his mouth on his sleeve. "Not bad. Not bad t'all." He takes another long drink and passes it on.

"Now, isn't this better than all us shooting at each other?" Ike says. "More neighborly and all?"

Yooko grunts. From the look in his eyes I get the feeling he'd prefer to be shooting. But there's an armed man out there somewhere in the darkness, he doesn't know where, and he doesn't want to chance anything he might regret.

Ike eats most all of the quail carcass, noisily chewing the bones and swallowing them. I'm pretty sure I even see a piece of wing, feathers and all, pass down his gullet. He wipes his hands on his trousers and burps. "Pass that bottle back on over here, now. Don't be selfish."

Yooko shakes his head. "No. Drink your own." He adds something in Yaqui which I'm reasonably sure isn't a compliment.

Ike's eyes narrow down. "Is that it, then? That's how this is going to play out?" I see his hand drift down near his gun. Still a good chance of all of them shooting each other.

Yooko takes another drink of the whiskey and gives it to one of his braves, deliberately bypassing Ike. Ike bristles, then says, "Have it your way." He goes to his horse and pulls a bottle of whiskey out of the saddlebags. He comes back to the fire and sits down.

"Godammit, Ike! You better not drink all that hooch without me!" comes a voice from out of the darkness.

"We drew straws and you lost!" Ike yells back. "Shut yer yap! You'll give your location away!"

"The hell with my location. How long I gotta sit out here in the dark anyway?"

Ike grumbles and takes another drink.

"What was that?" Luke yells.

"I said I'm thinking about it! Don't get your knickers in a twist!"

Ike grumbles some more and stares at the Yaqui braves. They're drinking and pretending he doesn't exist. Finally, Ike straightens up and yells, "Come on in then, Luke!"

There's some crashing in the bushes and another man appears. The first thing I notice is he's got no hat. His head looks strange without it, the top of his forehead a shocking white, the lower part and the rest of his face scorched brown. He's wearing this shiny vest with silver buttons and a neckerchief. The neckerchief is bright red with flowers patterned on it.

"Give me some of that bottle afore you drink it all!" he yelps.

15

"There's plenty left."

Luke sits down and looks at the Yaquis. His gaze fixes on Yooko. "Where'd you get that hat? I'll trade you for it."

Yooko takes my hat off and looks at it. He looks like a man admiring a beautiful object, turning it this way and that. Then he puts it back on. "Mine," he says.

"What do you want with that hat?" Luke says. "Injuns don't wear hats. It's like putting a dress on a dog. You ought to give it to me."

"Trade you for cloth." Yooko points at Luke's kerchief. "Gift for squaw."

"The hell you say!" Luke squawks. "I just got this. It's brand-spanking new. You want too much for a beat-up nasty old hat."

Hey, that's my hat you're talking about.

Yooko shakes his head. "No trade." He picks up the bottle and takes another drink.

"Serves you right for getting too close to that mule," Ike says, taking a drink. "I done told you he was ornery."

"How was I s'posed to know he'd eat my hat?" Luke grabs the bottle from Ike and takes a drink of his own. "Goddamned malicious critter is what he is."

"Just give him the neckerchief already," Ike says. "It ain't fit for a man to wear no how. Flowers all over it. What're you, some kind of dandy?"

"My girl gave it to me!" Luke protests. "A sign of her undying love. I cain't just toss it away."

"Then go about your day without a hat. Makes no difference to me," Ike says.

"God damn your eyes," Luke says, taking off the neckerchief and throwing it at Yooko. "You're cheating me. Taking unfair advantage of a man in need."

Yooko catches the neckerchief and tosses over the hat. It's a bad throw, and for an instant I think it's going to fall into the fire, but Luke snatches it just in time. Yooko ties the cloth around his neck, lifts his chin and shows the other braves, who nod and make approving noises.

"It's not much of a hat," Luke says, eyeing it doubtfully. "More like something you'd stick on a scarecrow than a man."

Okay, now I'm really starting to dislike this man.

Luke sniffs it. "It smells. Don't these Injuns ever wash their hair?"

If things get ugly, I'm definitely shooting him first.

5

The six of them settle in to some serious drinking then. As the bottles get lighter, the mood does too. There's yelling and laughing, even some snatches of song from Ike and Luke, though those usually end after a verse or two with the men arguing about what the words are. The drunker they get, the better I feel about my chances of pulling this off. At the rate they're going, I'll be able to walk in and take anything and everything I want.

Ike wanders off to take a piss, and when he gets back he says, "You know what this shindig needs? A game!"

Yooko looks up at him. His head wobbles and I notice his eyes kind of cross when he tries to focus on Ike. "Game?" he asks. One of his braves rattles off something, probably asking him what the crazy white man just said, and he shrugs.

"It's something you do for fun. You gents know what fun is, don't you?" Ike is still on his feet, weaving slightly.

"Fun," Yooko says, and nods vigorously. The other braves all start nodding too and a chorus of "Fun" floats up into the air.

"Here's how you play." Ike draws his knife. It's quite the pig sticker, with a blade about as long as his forearm. The Yaquis all look alarmed and hands reach for weapons.

"No, no!" Ike says, holding his other hand out to calm them. "It ain't like that. Here, Luke and I will show you." He turns to Luke. "Get up."

Luke looks up at him blearily. "What's that?"

"I want to show these savages how to play mumbly-peg. Get up."

"Mumbly-what?" Luke ponders this, then smiles real big. "Oh, you mean foot-sticker. Why sure enough, I'll help."

He clambers to his feet, loses his balance, and has to grab hold of a nearby sapling to keep from falling down.

"Now, the point of the game is to get as close to the other feller's foot as you can without sticking him," Ike says.

I shift my position so I can see better. This promises to be entertaining and I don't want to miss any of it.

"If you stick him, you lose. An' if he chickens out and moves his foot, *he* loses." Ike squints at Yooko. "You understand?"

Yooko and the others talk amongst themselves for a minute, then all four nod. They look excited at the prospect of this new game. My opinion of their general intelligence drops a few notches.

Ike takes hold of the pig sticker by the blade while Luke sets his feet. Ike closes one eye to aim, his tongue sticking out a little between his teeth.

Ike lets fly. Unfortunately, the knife doesn't stick in Luke's foot or anywhere else interesting. Surprisingly, it flies true and sticks in the ground only a couple inches from Luke's right foot.

"Gonna have to be a lot closer than that before you see me jump!" Luke hoots. "And now it's my turn." When he bends to pick up the knife he staggers sideways and almost falls into the fire.

This is better than those penny shows and it doesn't cost a thing.

Luke tries to close one eye to aim, but it proves too difficult for him. It takes too much fine muscle control and each time he ends up closing both eyes instead of just one. So he settles for putting his hand over one eye. None of this lack of coordination seems to bother Ike in the least. He stands there picking his teeth with a dirty fingernail, looking like a man waiting for the stagecoach to arrive.

Luke throws. The knife flashes in the firelight and sticks in the ground right next to Ike's boot, so close it looks like it shaved off a bit of leather.

Ike doesn't even flinch. "Huh," he says, and bends to retrieve the blade. "I'm done playing with you, boy. This is Ike's game and he don't lose."

"Bring it on, hoss!" Luke yells. "Not afraid of you!"

Ike throws the knife—

And it sticks square in Luke's foot. For a moment Luke just stands there staring at it. He looks up at Ike.

Then he starts laughing.

"Ha! I knew you was all bluster, Ike!" He turns a red, smiling face to the Yaquis. "I win!" When he pulls the knife out of his foot a little pool of blood appears on top of his boot, but he pays no attention to it.

"You care to try again, Ike? Or have you had enough?"

It turns out Ike hasn't had enough. He starts hollering challenges right back at Luke.

As for the Yaqui braves, well they fall all over themselves in their excitement to get in on this amazing new game they just learned. They pair up and commence to throwing knives at each other, passing the whiskey bottle and laughing.

I'm thinking none of them is right in the head.

A couple rounds go by with nothing more than minor flesh wounds and then one of the braves throws a knife that sticks right in Yooko's thigh. Everyone stops what they're doing and stares at it, like a two-headed calf just appeared in their midst.

Yooko starts laughing first. Ike joins in and the rest follow. Yooko's laughing so hard that when he pulls the knife out he loses his balance and falls down. Quite a lot of blood is running down his leg, but he doesn't seem to notice until one of the braves points it out to him.

Lying on the ground, still laughing, he takes off his new kerchief and ties it around his thigh. For some reason that starts a whole new round of laughter for everyone.

I feel like I've stumbled onto some kind of crazy ceremony that I don't understand. Is this really what whiskey does to people? Am *I* that dumb when I'm drunk?

The game peters out a while later. I count three people who are actively bleeding and two more who seem to have stopped bleeding. The drinking after that is interspersed now and then by one of them holding up his wound and showing it off like it's a trophy and the others laughing.

Finally, they settle down and begin dropping off to sleep. The fire dies down to a glimmer. The snoring competition begins.

I stand up and stretch some of the sand out of my joints. I head over to Yooko first. One of my pistols is gripped in his hand. The other has come out of his belt where it was tucked and is lying on the dirt. I pick that one up first, dust it off and check the loads.

I sweat a little prying the other one out of his hand. He doesn't stir until I've got it free, but then he grumbles in his sleep and starts fumbling around for it. Thinking quickly, I put a chunk of wood into his hand. His fingers close on it and that seems to make him happy because he settles down and goes back to snoring.

Next I go to Luke for my hat. He has it pulled down over his face and when I lift it up I get a start.

His eyes are open.

It takes a moment to realize that he's not seeing anything. He's just one of those strange people who sleeps with his eyes open. There was a cowboy on the Bar T did that sometimes.

Still, I don't like the feeling and I reach out and close his lids. It's not natural.

Ike's last. I want that gold dust he's carrying. It won't make up for the share of treasure from the temple of Totec that I didn't get—not by a long shot—but it'll sure enough help.

I crouch down beside him. He's lying on his back, his mouth open, his arms down by his sides. Real careful I reach down inside his coat—

His eyes snap open and fix on me. They widen as he recognizes me. "You!" he hisses.

He starts grabbing iron and I club him in the temple with the butt of my gun. I don't shoot because I'm still hoping to keep this quiet. If I knock him out quick, I might be able to get out of here without rousing the others.

But old Ike has an iron skull. The gun butt skips off his head and doesn't do a thing to slow him down.

He brings his gun up and I slap it aside. He loses hold of it, but before he does it goes off, the bullet tearing through the trees overhead.

General pandemonium breaks out.

"I'm gonna kill you!" Ike howls. I'm standing, trying to back away when he sits up, lunges forward and bites me on the leg.

It hurts. I crack him on the head again and he's losing blood from a scalp wound now, but it doesn't seem to bother him all that much.

Meanwhile, Yooko responds. He leaps to his feet with a bloodcurdling yell, brings his gun up and fires at me point blank.

Except that he's not holding a gun. He's holding a stick and he hesitates, looking down at it in confusion.

I start to swing my gun around to bring him down, but Ike chooses that moment to pull his teeth out of my leg and go for my arm. My shot goes wild, but it brings Yooko out of his daze and he leaps over the fire and throws himself at me.

I manage to duck under his charge, twist and pivot while he's on top of me, and use his own momentum to toss him down on top of Luke, who's just climbing up out of sleep, dirt and leaves in his hair, looking around in confusion.

Yooko lands on top of Luke and they both go down in a pile.

The other braves are having a harder time shaking off the large quantities of whiskey they drank. One jumps up, trips, and falls into the fire, where he starts thrashing around, spreading coals everywhere, some of which get into the tall grasses. The fire starts to spread.

The other two start shooting without examining their targets too closely first. The first one's shot goes wild. The other one's doesn't, and his friend goes down with a leg wound.

Ike has gone back to biting again. I shake him off and when he tries to get up I kick him in the chest. He falls back and gets tangled up in Luke and Yooko who for some reason have started punching each other.

Time to hightail it out of here.

I kick a mess of coals and bits of burning wood at the brave who's still on his feet. I snap off a quick shot at Ike, though in the general confusion I can't tell if I hit him.

And I get the hell out of there.

6

I never do see any sign of pursuit from either the Yaquis or Ike and his idiot partner. Maybe they all bled to death from throwing knives at each other.

Coyote and I head north for the border. I'm still broke but I have my pistols and my hat back. That's what counts. Luke was right about one thing. The hat does smell. But I reckon that's from being on his ugly head. I'll dunk it in a river if I ever see one with water in it.

It's about the middle of the afternoon and I'm coming up on about where the border should be—no one really knows where, exactly, it is, not even the two governments involved—when I see someone familiar in the distance.

This is not a happy occurrence. I don't want to see him. And he probably doesn't want to see me. My first thought is to run, but that'll just make him chase me. He won't care if I get across the border either. My best bet is to face up and talk to him. We parted on good enough terms last time. Maybe we still are.

I stop, hook my leg around the saddle horn, and settle in to wait. It's times like these I wish I smoked cigarettes, so I could be casually smoking one when he comes up, maybe blow a smoke ring or two. But I tried them a couple times and they made me sick.

I don't have to wait long. He's already seen me and he and his men all come up at a nice, easy lope. His men are as rough looking as ever, scars, tattoos, missing body parts. They're former criminals, every one of them. Wearing the uniforms of the Mexican Rurales doesn't change that.

The men part when they get close and he emerges from their midst. He's riding that big chestnut stallion of his. The horse is probably twice Coyote's height. Coyote hates horses that are taller than him. Well, to be accurate, he hates all horses. But he *especially* hates tall horses. He lays his ears back and bares his teeth.

"Easy there, brother. Don't do anything foolish and get me killed," I tell him in a low voice. To the approaching rider I say, "Afternoon, Colonel Kosterlitzky. What brings you up this way?"

The Colonel looks me over before responding. His dark eyes are piercing and I feel an urge to confess to things I haven't done. He's an imposing man—ramrod straight, military uniform with braid on the shoulders, a saber hanging by his side—and widely feared on both sides of the border. The men he and his Rurales set out to catch, they generally catch. Some even survive the trip to prison.

"You survived your journey to the temple of Totec," he says. There's almost no trace of Russian accent in his voice. But I can see his Cossack heritage in the way he holds himself, the tone of voice that says he expects to be heard and obeyed.

"It was close a couple times."

"I see no treasure. I trust the General did not get his hands on it?"

A little chill goes through me, the way he says that. It's a question, but also a reminder. When last we parted he made it very clear how he felt about the General getting hold of the treasure. Something about personally hunting me down if I let it happen. It seems the General had plans for that treasure, plans that involved revolution and assassination.

"He had his hands on it," I say. "But not for very long."

"Can I tell President Diaz that he no longer need concern himself with de la Cruz?"

"You can."

"What happened to him?"

I remember the last time I saw General Rafael Santiago Dominguez de la Cruz, the things holding him down on that sacrificial altar. "He ran into some friends and couldn't get away."

Kosterlitzky nods. "He was not happy about the mess you made of his hacienda. Was it necessary to use that much dynamite?"

I scratch my cheek. "It seemed like it at the time."

"I must remember never to invite you to my home, at least not without properly searching you."

"You have a home?" I can only picture Kosterlitzky out here, riding after the bad guys.

"Of course. Everyone has a home. I am not an animal."

"A wife? Kids?"

He frowns to let me know I've gone too far, that he does not condone such familiarity. I wonder briefly if I will be 'shot while trying to escape'. Or maybe I'll get an offer to join the Rurales. The kind I can't refuse.

"It is not that kind of home," he says somberly. He looks around. "You seem to have lost your two companions."

"Or they lost me." I know I sound bitter when I say it, and I don't care. I *am* bitter. "I don't want to talk about it."

"I am not interested in hearing. I only wished to know if the young lady was well."

"Last time I saw her she looked just fine."

"And now you return to the United States, no?"

Relief goes through me. I think this means he's going to let me go. "That's the plan."

"Good. It is probably better that you leave Mexico. I am thinking that you cause problems where you go. You have done me a small favor. I would not wish to return it by shooting you."

"That's exactly how I feel." I unhook my leg and pick up the reins. Then something occurs to me.

"There's a man, name of Ike Clanton."

Kosterlitzky nods. "I know this name. There was a problem between him and the Earps in Tombstone a while ago. A shootout."

"You *know* about that?"

"It is quite famous and Mexico is not the end of the world."

I guess I should be happy he doesn't know about my part in it.

"I saw Ike last night, south of here." One of the Colonel's impressive eyebrows rises fractionally. "He was selling guns to some Yaqui Indians. Thought you might like to know."

That gets his interest. The Mexican government has been fighting with the Yaquis for a long time. More guns isn't something they want the Yaquis to have.

A few minutes later I ride away all smiles. Not only did I earn a few points with Kosterlitzky, but I shouldn't have to worry about Ike for a while.

Or ever again.

7

It's afternoon when I ride into Tombstone. It feels like a lifetime has gone by since I was last here, but the town looks the same. Dusty, sagging, unpainted buildings, signs creaking in the wind.

Maybe it was a lifetime. A lot happened after we left here. Getting chased by the Scalphunters, captured by Kosterlitzky, blowing up the General's hacienda. And let's not forget Totec's temple. Was that thing really a god? I hope I never find out.

I'm broke, so I don't head for the OK Corral. Nor do I head for the boarding house where I first ran into the Clantons and the McLaurys. Instead I mosey on down the main street, trying not to draw too much attention, but keeping my eyes peeled for Doc Holliday.

I told Doc I'd come back and catch him up on what happened. But I'm a little worried about the Earps, Wyatt especially. I helped him and his brothers out of a tight spot, but I'm still a wanted man and he's a marshal. Those two things go together about as good as a polecat and a possum.

To my surprise, it's easy to find Doc.

He's coming out of a saloon, a bottle in one hand and a glass in the other. He's wearing his usual, a long, black coat over a black waistcoat and a white shirt. He's got on a skinny bow tie and his pearl-handled revolver is tied down. He holds the door open. "Put it right over there, boys." He points to a spot on the saloon's wooden porch.

Two men come out carrying a table. Right behind them is a man sporting suspenders and a bright red shirt. He's hugely fat, easily the fattest man I've ever seen, and I'm immediately fascinated by him. I've hardly ever even seen a fat person and none while growing up in Pa-Gotzin-Kay, where we spent our first few years trying not to starve to death.

The fat man storms over to Doc. "What are you doing? You can't take my table outside!"

"Too late," Doc says cheerfully. "I already did."

"I won't allow it," the fat man bellows. To the two who are carrying the table he says, "You take it back inside right this minute!"

The two men look from him to Doc. Doc doesn't say anything, just shakes his head. "Sorry, Ralph," one of them says, and they put the table down and scurry back inside.

The door opens again and a man comes out carrying a chair.

"My chair," Doc says. "Right on time."

"It's not your chair!" Ralph bellows. "No furniture is to leave the establishment."

"But it hasn't left," Doc says calmly, taking a seat and setting bottle and glass down on the table. "This fine porch here belongs to you, doesn't it?"

"That's not what I meant." Ralph's extra chin wobbles with every movement of his head. I wonder what he ate to get so fat. I wonder if it took him a long time.

"Don't get so worked up, Ralph," Doc says. "It's bad for your health. Take it from me. I'm a doctor."

"You're not a doctor, you're a dentist."

"Aren't they the same thing?"

"Not at all. You wouldn't know what to do if a man came to you with the yellow fever, or a bullet in his leg, would you?"

"Sure I would," Doc says reasonably. "I'd look at all his teeth very carefully, and I'd pull any that looked like they were going septic." For a moment Ralph can only stare at him, his eyes bulging, his cheeks getting redder. I wonder if he's going to explode on the spot.

"Be reasonable, Ralph. It's hot in your saloon. So hot I was considering skipping my afternoon whiskey and retiring to my room for a nap. And, lest you forget, I don't spend money while I'm napping."

That reels Ralph right back in. I can see him working over this new bit of evidence he hadn't considered before.

"It's much more pleasant out here," Doc continues. "Especially with the shade from the fine roof you erected over this fine porch." It's not a fine roof. The boards are warped so bad they're curled up like spider legs in a fire. But it does offer at least some shade from the hot sun.

"Go on back inside and tend to your fine establishment. I promise I won't take the table anywhere. Hell, I might even bring it back inside when I'm done with it."

Ralph mutters something and storms back inside.

"Still making friends, I see," I say.

Doc looks up and sees me sitting there on Coyote. His face lights up in a big smile. "Hot damn! If it isn't my amigo Ace!" He's loud and some people walking by on the street turn and look at us.

"Good to see you too, Doc."

He looks Coyote over and his smile fades away. "Did you fall on hard times, then?"

"What makes you say that?"

"I think that's the ugliest horse I've ever seen."

I want to deny it, but he's right. Coyote *is* ugly. Except not to me. "You're just saying that because you can't see Coyote's heart," I tell Doc. "If you could see that, you'd know he's the handsomest horse that ever lived."

I lean forward so I can whisper in Coyote's ear. "Don't let it bother you, brother. He doesn't know any better."

Doc looks skeptical, but he says, "Well, climb on down off your handsome horse then and set a spell with me, won't you?"

"I believe I will."

"I'll go get you a chair and a glass."

Doc disappears into the saloon and I get down and loop Coyote's reins loosely over the hitching rail. There's already another horse at the rail, a big, roan gelding. The roan flattens his ears, making sure Coyote knows this is *his* hitching rail and Coyote better mind his place.

He doesn't know how wrong he is.

Before I can stop him, Coyote lunges at him and bites him hard on the neck. The roan whinnies and side hops as far as his reins will allow, the whites of his eyes showing. As a big horse, he's probably used to pushing other horses around with no trouble. What he doesn't know is that being big just makes Coyote hate him even more.

I take hold of Coyote's bridle before he gets carried away and starts seriously stomping the gelding. "Take it easy on him,

Coyote. He doesn't know any better and I don't feel like fighting his owner right now." Coyote flares his nostrils at me. "I mean it, Coyote. Not right now."

He shakes his head out of my grip, but he doesn't go after the gelding again. The gelding meanwhile has moved as far down the hitching rail as he can and is watching Coyote like a mouse watching a snake.

8

Doc comes out with my glass and chair. He sets them down and pumps my hand. "Ace Lone Wolf, as I live and breathe." He starts coughing and has to bring out his hanky. His coughing fit over, he looks at the blood on the cloth before putting it away. "Well, as I live anyway."

We sit down. "You look good, Doc. All healed up from that gut wound." That's not entirely true. Doc looks a bit pale and his clothes are loose on him.

He waves it off and pours me some whiskey. "I told you it was nothing but a scratch. No way a skunk like Ike Clanton is killing me. If a man's going to shoot me down, it's going to be a man of quality."

I take a drink of the whiskey and for a moment I just sit there and enjoy the burn. Doc drinks good stuff. "Funny you should mention him. I saw Ike a while back. In Mexico."

"Do tell," Doc replies. "So Wyatt hasn't caught up to him yet, then."

"How come he didn't hang?"

"It was that damned jury. They let him off, if you can believe that. Said it was just a gunfight and a man has a right to defend himself."

I remember Billy Clanton up on that roof with his rifle, ready to cut us down. "What about the ambush?"

"Bah. I said the same thing. Ike claimed Billy was up there to make sure nobody tried to take advantage. Nothing would have happened if you hadn't started shooting at him first."

"They *believed* that?"

"That they did. Durned fools. You should have seen Wyatt afterwards. He was madder than a hornet in a hoosegow. No one could talk him down. He turned in his badge, gathered a few friends, and took off chasing Ike a couple days later. I would've gone, but I was still laid up at the time."

I believe that. Doc's a loyal friend, as loyal as they come. At least this means I don't have to worry about running into Wyatt.

Doc pours me some more whiskey and leans over the table, fixing me with those intense eyes of his. "What happened? Did you find the temple? Did you save the girl's father?"

It takes a while to tell him the whole story. Doc interrupts me now and then to whoop it up. Another bottle of whiskey shows up. By the time I get to telling him how it all ended I'm drunk enough that it hardly hurts at all.

When I'm finished, Doc shakes his head. "How I envy you, out there roaming the wilderness, facing the worst it has to offer with your gun in your hand. You are the model of the modern Western man."

"You think so? I never really thought of it like that," I say. Probably because I've been busy feeling like a damned fool. I sit up a little straighter in my chair.

"I do, I do. Sure, this little adventure didn't work out the way you planned, but I'm sure the next one will."

"I wouldn't mind that."

"What's next?" Doc asks.

"I don't know. I'm dead broke. Maybe I can get on as a hand on one of the ranches."

"No." Doc shakes his head vigorously. "I won't hear of it. You're a man of adventure, Ace! You need to be out there, running free like a wild mustang."

I have to admit, the whole running free sounds a lot better than punching cows. As fine as his words are, though, they don't put any coins in my pocket. "I should at least find some work to get by on."

"Let me put my mind to it. I must know someone who could use your considerable skills."

About then a rowdy gust of wind blows through town and here comes a dust devil, right down the middle of the street. It's a big one, carrying tumbleweeds, trash, a few hats. I might even see a cat stuck in there, but I can't be sure. It sends everyone running but the two of us. Doc grabs hold of the bottle and pulls it close. I pull my hat down over my eyes and hunker down.

When it's gone by, Doc squints at the sky and says, "We should probably be getting ourselves inside. Looks like it's fixing to blow."

He's right. While we were sitting here talking some big old thunderheads have built to the south, like they do this time of summer. Lightning is flickering in their depths and a thick wall of rain is visible underneath them.

"We could be in for a real gully washer," I say.

We pick up the table and hustle it indoors. None too soon, either. The first fat raindrops hit right after we get inside.

"See?" Doc says to Ralph. "I told you I'd bring your table back, didn't I?"

"You better not have scratched it up," Ralph growls from his spot behind the bar. He points at me. "And don't bring him in here. No Injuns in the bar. It says so on the sign."

"He's not an Injun," Doc replies. "He's a half-breed and he's with me."

"That don't change anything. I won't have the likes of him in here fouling up the place."

With those last words something changes. Everyone in the place can instantly feel it. Doc freezes. Slowly he sets the whiskey bottle down on the table and turns toward Ralph, who takes a step back and fetches up against the shelves behind the bar.

"You might want to reconsider your words, sir," Doc says in a low voice. I notice he's flipped his long coat back, exposing the pistol tied down to his leg. "I don't appreciate folks speaking ill of my friends."

Ralph swallows and tries to lick his lips with a tongue gone suddenly dry. "I might have misspoke."

"And…?"

"And what?" The bar is completely quiet, everyone watching the drama unfold.

"And an apology for my friend. His name is Ace, so you can make it personal and everything."

Ralph swallows again. "My apologies, Ace. No offense intended."

"None taken."

"Well," Doc says cheerfully, just like that back to his old self, "see how much pleasanter the day is when we're all civilized?"

The room gets really bright all of a sudden as a lightning bolt hits nearby, probably right out front in the street. The thunderclap hits right after, loud enough and strong enough to shake the heart in your chest.

The thunderclap dies away and the rain starts coming down, sheets of it. A man hustles for the doors. Probably it's the owner of the roan gelding, going to catch his horse before he runs all the way to Mexico. I'm not worried. Even if Coyote runs off, he'll come back.

I hope. At least he has every time so far.

"It appears we came inside just in time," Doc says. He makes a show of looking me over. "Although, perhaps the shower would have done you some bit of good. You are a touch pungent, my friend, and your hat is so dirty that I believe it could be used to bait rat traps."

"What's wrong with my hat? It's fine. Finally broken in right so it's comfortable."

"It's your head," he replies. "One thing I've had in the back of my mind since I met you, Ace, a question I'd like to ask you. That is, if you don't mind me inquiring after your heritage some?"

"Go ahead."

"I assumed that your father is where the Apache in you comes from, that he carried off your mother at some point and that led, by and by, to you. But certain things you have said have made me think this is not the truth of it."

"My mother found my father near dead of a gunshot wound. She brought him back to our clan and nursed him back to health. Grandfather objected, but my mother is not a woman who takes no easily." I smile, thinking of my mother. Because of the whiskey, I come close to telling him more, how my grandfather was the famous Apache chief Cochise, but I have learned that it is better to keep that information to myself.

"And you grew up with the Apaches then?"

I nod. "My father ran off years ago."

Before Doc can ask another question, a man walks up to the table, leans down to get a good look at me, and says, "It's you, ain't it?"

34

I don't know what to say. While it's true that I am me, I'm not sure he knows that. "Do I know you?"

"No, but I know you." He's got a big, red beard that frames his round face. He's wearing overalls and a big, straw hat that's worn completely through in a few spots. His cheeks are red from drinking. "You're the feller what shot Billy Clanton off the roof of the mercantile!"

I wish he wouldn't have said it so loud. Between Doc's natural loudness, the business with the bartender, and now this man, my plans for keeping a low profile in this town don't seem to be working out all that well.

"I saw it all and that was fine shooting!" the man hoots. He makes guns with his hands like a child would do and starts pretending to shoot up into the corner of the room. "Pow, pow! Pow, pow!"

He turns and starts shooting across the room. "Then you shot old Frank McLaury. Pow, pow! I never seen the like."

Everyone in the place is looking at me. I want to leave. "I don't remember all that well, truth be told."

"It don't matter, because I do. I'll never forget." The man taps his temple with one finger. "It's all right here. Let me buy you a drink, mister."

Okay. That doesn't sound too bad.

He buys me a drink and for some reason that starts some kind of stampede. Outside the rain is pouring down and inside they're all but throwing liquor at me. Everyone wants to buy me a drink. I don't understand it, but after a few drinks I give up and settle down to enjoy it.

Time passes and I get good and sauced. Most of what happens next is sort of blurry, though I do remember at one point someone saying that I owe them all a shooting demonstration, so they can see for themselves how great I am with a gun.

That seems like a fine idea to me and I get up out of my chair and stagger out onto the porch. Men crowd around me and start throwing items up into the air for me to shoot at. Of course, by then it's dark and it's still raining hard so I can't see if I hit a single thing, but they cheer with every shot anyway and so I don't worry about it.

After that the blurriness comes back, worse than ever, and eventually it all goes blank.

9

"Is this the feller you were talking about? He don't look like much to me."

"He's looked better, I allow."

The words come from far away and through a haze of pain. My head feels like a team of men have been at work inside it with pickaxes. I try to swallow, but my tongue is bigger than my mouth and it feels like my cheeks are full of sawdust.

"Come on, Ace. Get up. I got you a job." It's Doc.

"Graaagh," I say. I'm not sure what it's supposed to mean. I don't think there's a word in Apache or English for how I feel.

"I don't believe I need a shotgun that bad." It's the first speaker. The voice is rough and gravelly, not someone I know.

I risk a peek. Sunlight stabs me in the eye and the pain in my head doubles. I close my eye again.

"Now don't give up on him so soon, Lou," Doc says. "Ace is a fine gunman and a fine man. You need him. You told me yourself this run is dangerous, what with the outlaw gangs and renegade Indians and all."

"He might be able to handle a gun, but he clearly can't handle his liquor." Lou sounds disgusted. Worse than that, he sounds doubtful. I decide I've had enough.

"Hold on a minute," I say, rolling over onto my side. At least, that's what I mean to say. My tongue's so swollen I can't get any of the words out and it ends up sounding like someone is choking a cat.

I hold my hand up and Doc grabs on and pulls me to my feet. Blinking, I look around. I'm out in the street in front of the saloon. The sun has recently risen. Behind Doc I see a woman walking by, holding her skirts up to keep them out of the mud. The look she gives me speaks loudly about her views on drunks who pass out in the street.

"What happened?" I ask.

"You were a star," Doc replies. "But you forgot to say no to that last glass of whiskey."

I see my hat lying on the ground. It's not easy to pick it up. I almost fall down twice. The hat's looking extra disreputable this morning. I slap some of the dust off it, but it doesn't seem to make any difference.

Once it's on my head, I look at Lou. His hat's huge and brown and the front brim is folded up tight against the crown. I never understood why someone would do that to a hat. Why turn the brim up like that, where it won't do a thing to protect against sun or rain?

Lou himself is a few inches shorter than me and probably twenty pounds heavier. A permanent tobacco stain runs from one corner of his mouth down to his chin. He has no beard or facial hair at all, not even any stubble, which is unusual out here where razors are scarce. His brown hair is thick and curly and streaked with gray. He's wearing a black eye patch and the look I see in the other eye is not a friendly one.

"Lou, meet Ace. Ace, meet Lou."

I stick out my hand in the white man fashion and Lou takes it. His hand is coarse and thick and his grip is strong.

"Doc says you can shoot. Is this true?"

I nod. The motion makes me feel like throwing up.

"You get drunk like that every night?"

"I hope not."

"You're not going to jabber on all day, are you? I can't stand a man who can't shut up."

"Ace here is more the strong, silent type," Doc says.

"I've got a wagonload of cargo to haul north," Lou says. "Could be someone riding shotgun would come in handy. You think you're up to the job?"

Right now I don't feel up to anything. Even falling down seems like too much work.

"Just say yes, Ace," Doc says. "You said you need a job."

"Okay. I'll do it."

"We're leaving in twenty minutes. Grab your gear and be at the OK Corral." Lou turns and stumps off.

Doc stares after him, then turns back to me. "A magnificent woman, don't you think?"

It takes a moment for the words to penetrate. "Wait. Why'd you call Lou a woman?"

"Because that's what she is. I take it this means you didn't notice."

I still feel pretty fogged up. All I can manage is "*What*?"

"Don't feel too bad. I imagine not very many people notice. People see what they expect to see. Someone who dresses like that, who's also an accomplished mule skinner, well, he must be a man. That's what they expect, and that's what they see."

I'm still stuck. "Lou's a *woman*?"

"Ace, Ace, you're a little slow this morning, aren't you?" he chides me.

I peer after the receding figure. Sure looks like a man to me. "I still don't know..."

"Trust me. I'm an expert on these things."

"An expert on telling men from women? You've seen this before?"

"It's not a common thing, I'll grant that. But it happens."

"You're having fun with me, aren't you? This is some kind of white man humor that I don't understand."

Doc claps me on the shoulder and laughs. "It's funny, all right. Just not for the reason you think. Don't worry. You and Lou are going to get along just fine. Lou's quite the character, once you crack through the shell."

I raise an eyebrow at him. "Are we talking about the same person?" I'm thinking there's nothing *but* shell to Lou.

"I'm sure you'll have plenty of stories to tell when you get back." He takes my elbow and starts moving me down the street. "Let's move along now. Lou hates waiting and I'm sure you don't want to make a bad impression your first day on the job."

Partway there he looks at me. "Don't let on though, okay? Clearly Lou doesn't want people to know, so let us not be the ones who spill the proverbial beans."

10

Doc waves goodbye as the wagon pulls out of town, Lou driving, me on the seat next to him—uh, her. That's an idea that's going to take some getting used to. I take a sideways peek at Lou, trying to see what Doc sees.

I don't know. Maybe Doc is wrong on this one. Lou looks like a regular man to me.

"You done staring at me yet?" Lou growls.

"I wasn't staring."

"The hell you weren't. You looking for something in particular, or you just the starin' type?"

"I was just...I was..." I cast about for something to say that makes even a little bit of sense. Then it hits me. "I've never seen anyone with only one eye before."

"Is that so?" Lou leans over close and pulls up the eye patch suddenly, shoves the lost eye right in my face. "Whaddya think?"

I think right there I almost lost whatever's still sloshing around inside my gut. What's underneath the eye patch is a terrible, grisly mess. "How did it happen?"

"Mule kicked me."

"Sorry about that." I don't know what else to say.

"No you're not."

I have no answer to that. Lou's right. I just said it because that's what I learned you're supposed to say around white people.

"I used to be a whole lot prettier before."

"You did?"

"Sure. I had all the girls panting after me." Lou gives me a dead pan expression. I decide he—Lou has to be a man, whatever Doc said—is messing with me.

We ride in silence for a couple of hours. I take out my handkerchief and wipe down my Winchester lever-action 1873. The Spencer rifle is in the bed of the wagon with the rest of my gear, including my saddle. It's more of a long-range gun, while the Winchester rifle is better for up-close work, faster, shorter.

Lou looks at the rifle and says, "You any good with that?"

"I can shoot."

Lou grunts. "Losing an eye didn't help my shooting much. That's why I carry Betsy now." Lou reaches under the seat and pulls out a double-barreled shotgun. "Betsy don't care how many eyes I have."

I turn to check on Coyote, who is trotting along behind us. He's pretty sore at me this morning, probably for leaving him out in the rain all night. He tried to bite part of my ear off when I was pulling off his saddle to put it in the wagon.

"Ain't you worried your horse is going to run off, no lead rope or nothing?"

"He doesn't belong to me. If he wants to run off, he can."

"Did you steal him?"

"No, I paid for him."

"Then why'd you say he don't belong to you?"

I think about it, how I fought Matthews when he was going to kill Coyote. I don't feel like telling Lou about it. "It's a long story."

Lou grunts. I get the feeling he wouldn't want to hear about it anyway.

A few more hours pass and I ask, "Where are we going?"

Lou pulls a plug of tobacco out of his shirt pocket, bites off a chunk and commences to chewing it. A couple minutes pass as he works the thing down, getting it to where it will ride comfortable in his cheek. He spits a brown glob over the side and finally responds. "North."

Sure. That's helpful.

The wagon is big, a good fifteen feet long, with a four-mule team pulling it. There are four long, wooden crates in the bed. "What's in the crates?"

Lou shrugs. "I dunno. I'm not paid to know. I'm paid to deliver and that's what I aim to do." He spits over the side. "Thought you said you weren't going to talk the whole time."

Lou doesn't say a word the rest of the day. Not to me, anyway. He does talk to the mules, mostly to one of the front ones, who he calls Old Nibs, which sounds like a foolish name to me, but I don't say anything. He seems to like Old Nibs better than people. That much I understand, feeling much the same way about Coyote.

He says things to the mule like "How's it up there, Old Nibs? You making hay?"

Or "You reckon it will rain tonight, Old Nibs?"

Every time after he asks the mule a question he pauses, just like he's listening for an answer. I wonder if Lou lost more than his eye when that mule kicked him. I wonder if it was Old Nibs who kicked him.

Like all mule skinners, Lou uses the bull whip steadily. Mules are naturally stubborn, lazy animals and they don't seem all that happy about pulling heavy loads around. Without steady encouragement they'd do a whole lot of nothing. Lou provides that encouragement with the whip. Most of the time he just makes it pop by their ears, but when that doesn't work he pops them on the rump, enough to raise up a bit of dust and remind them to pick up their feet.

He's good with that whip, too. Along about midafternoon a horse fly lands on Old Nibs' flank and proceeds to help himself to some mule blood. Lou snaps the whip and the horse fly falls dead.

11

We make camp around dark. Lou doesn't say a word to me the whole evening except when I ask what's in the bowl he hands me after he whips us up some grub.

"Hog and hominy."

I poke it with my fork. The burned meat is the hog part, I guess. Which means the mushy stuff that looks somewhat like corn that someone already chewed must be hominy. The hominy tastes like a whole lot of nothing, but I keep that observation to myself. It may taste like nothing, but it's still a whole lot better than nothing.

The next morning Lou hands me a bowl of the same thing as the night before, except that there's no hog this time and the hominy has gone and gotten all cold and sticky, which definitely does not improve the flavor.

"You have any salt?" I ask. Lou stops chewing and gives me a long look. "You know, for flavor?"

"You saying you don't like it?"

"No, no. I'm not saying that at all. I'm just saying a little salt wouldn't be bad."

"No. Salt ain't part of the deal."

"Speaking of deal, what *is* the deal? How much are you paying me for this job? How long is it going to take?"

"It takes as long as it takes," he says with a shrug, shoveling in another forkful of the glop. "Pay's twenty dollars."

That doesn't sound too bad.

"Less the cost of the vittles."

"I have to *pay* for this?"

Lou smiles. It's not a friendly smile. "No, you don't. You could go hungry."

"Or I could shoot something. How about one of those mules?" I'm not too happy with them right now. I wasn't paying close enough attention when I first got up and Old Nibs kicked me in the leg.

"Don't be sore at the mules cuz you're too dumb to get out of the way." He takes another bite. "Mule's tough anyway. You'd complain about that too."

"I'm not complaining about the food. I'm complaining about having to pay for it."

"I thought you redskins were s'posed to be tough. I guess living amongst the pale faces has made you soft."

I start to protest, then give it up. Maybe I have gone soft. I finish off the hominy and help Lou hitch up the mules.

Old Nibs watches me close the whole time. From his expression I can tell he's laughing at me. He's a patient old bastard. He'll wait and he'll watch, figuring sooner or later I'll be careless again and he can give me another wallop.

I grab hold of his bit and pull his head close. "You got lucky. It's not going to happen again."

He rolls his eye at me and clicks his teeth together a couple times. He's definitely enjoying this.

"Stop playing with Old Nibs and let's go," Lou growls as he climbs onto the wagon seat. "We're burning daylight."

We roll out of camp and head for the mountains to the north. Wagons are slow, unpleasant devices, with none of the natural rhythm and flow of a horse. By midday I'm convinced they were invented to torture a man. Every bump in the road bounces me into the air. Every dip is like taking a fall. The seat is hard and filled with splinters. I have at least two in my ass and no way am I asking Lou for help in getting them out.

Finally I can't take it anymore. "You mind if I ride my horse instead?" I ask Lou.

Lou spits and turns his one eye on me. At first he just stares at me. Looking at him, I'm completely convinced that Doc is dead wrong. There's no way Lou is a woman. No way.

"You hired on as shotgun. Shotgun rides shotgun. Or he don't get paid."

"What am I doing here that I couldn't do on my horse? Hell, if I was on my horse I could scout on ahead."

"Shotgun rides shotgun." Lou turns back to the mules and pops the bull whip over their heads.

"If I'm riding shotgun, shouldn't I be carrying the shotgun?"

Lou gives me another sour look. He's clearly not in the mood for much of anything. "You always complain this much?"

"I'm just saying, it seems like the man riding shotgun should be holding the shotgun. You know, since you're so fixed on the whole shotgun thing."

Lou picks a piece of tobacco out of his teeth and turns back to the mules. "How you doing up there, Old Nibs?"

Old Nibs swivels his ears but otherwise keeps his thoughts to himself.

"You know what the word crotchety means, don't you?" I ask Lou.

"You know what 'shut the hell up' means, don't you?" he replies.

I ignore him and continue on. "I never really knew what that word meant before I met you. Now I know. It means Lou."

Lou pulls the whip back to pop one of the mules who's not pulling his share. But this time, as the whip snaps forward, it catches the brim of my hat and my hat goes flying off.

"Hey! What was that for?"

"Oops," Lou says. "Guess I was just being crotchety."

I jump down and pick up my hat. It's not looking too good these days. I have to get a new one when this job is over.

I climb back onto the wagon. "Anyone ever tell you you're downright unlikable?" I tell Lou.

Lou scratches his armpit. "Nope. Everybody likes me. 'Cept you, of course. But you don't count."

"How do you figure?"

"You're one of them fellers who's just never happy with anything."

Unbelievable. Am I really having this conversation? "I'm done talking to you. You're plumb crazy as a bedbug."

Lou smiles, showing stained, yellow teeth. "Best thing you said all day." He pops the whip over one of the mules and starts humming to himself.

I settle in for more hours on that miserable seat. Maybe I'll get lucky and someone will try to rob us.

12

We make camp at the base of the mountains. I help Lou unhitch the wagon and Lou hobbles three of the mules, but lets Old Nibs graze freely. I build a small fire and Lou starts cooking. When it's ready I serve myself a bowl.

"Oh look, hog and hominy again," I say. "A body can't get enough hog and hominy."

Lou ignores me and commences to eating.

"You eat this every day, don't you?" No answer. "I think I know why you're so crotchety. If I had to eat this every day, I'd be crotchety too."

Lou looks up. "You got a point? Or you just flappin' your gums?"

"It's called making friendly conversation."

"No it ain't." Lou goes back to eating and staring into the fire.

I stare at the gluey mass and the pieces of burned pork in my bowl. How many days am I going to have to eat this? I shove some in, hoping it's better this time around. But it isn't. I put the bowl down.

"Now that we're best friends..." I pause, watching for a response from Lou, but there isn't one. "We *are* best friends, aren't we?"

That gets me a response. The look he gives me is positively black.

"Since we're best friends—" I can see the way those last two words make him wince "—I'm going to give you a gift. Are you excited to know what it is?" Lou kind of shakes his head in disgust, shoves another bite in his mouth and works it around. I dig around in my saddlebags and pull out a length of leather piggin' string.

"I'm going to teach you how to make a snare. With a snare, you can catch a rabbit. You like rabbit, don't you?" Still Lou ignores me.

"Of course you do. Everybody likes rabbit. You know the best thing about rabbit?"

I wait. After the silence stretches on a bit I say, "Lou!"

Lou looks up reluctantly.

"It's called friendly conversation. Remember?"

"Horse shit."

"Well, I've never heard it called that, but maybe where you're from it is. Anyway, the best thing about rabbit is it isn't burned pig." I tie the piggin' string into a loop, make a couple of twists, and hold it up.

"Here's your rabbit. Or it will be, come morning. You want to know how to set it?"

Lou picks up a piece of the burned hog and bites into it.

"I guess that means no." I stand up. "I'm going to wander off now and find a rabbit run. You wait here."

I start to walk off. Suddenly there is a frightened whinny from the darkness. I pull a gun and take off running. I can do this because I've been careful not to stare into the fire while Lou and I were having our friendly conversation. Fire kills your night vision.

Lou jumps up and comes after me, but he's been staring into the fire and he makes it about three steps before he trips over my saddle and pitches down on his face.

I crash into the bushes. I know Coyote's whinny and that wasn't him. Three of the mules are hobbled right near the fire, so it has to be Old Nibs. That explains all the thrashing and swearing I hear from Lou behind me. He's powerful fond of that mule.

I break out of the bushes into a clearing. On the far side is Old Nibs. There's something light-colored on his back. Something flashing lots of claws and teeth.

A cougar.

I start shouting and shooting at the same time. Cats don't like loud noises. That's why I'm shouting.

They also don't like being shot. It's hard to shoot in the bad light and with the two animals thrashing around, but at least one shot lands.

The cougar screams. Another shot and the cougar decides it's too hot here and takes off.

"Don't you shoot Old Nibs!" Lou yells from behind me. "Don't you shoot him!"

I run over to the mule. Old Nibs is understandably pretty upset and it takes a minute to get a hold of his halter and get him calmed down.

By then Lou comes crashing out of the bushes. "Old Nibs!" he yells. "Is he okay?"

I can see there's blood running down his back, but not much else. "Let's get him back to the fire."

At the fire it looks bad at first, lots of blood everywhere, but a closer look shows me the wounds aren't deep. Some of the blood probably isn't his.

Lou is carrying on in the most surprising way. The man is practically blubbering, hugging the mule, petting him, talking to him in a strangely high voice.

All at once it hits me. Doc was right. Lou *is* a woman.

13

All at once Lou seems to realize that I'm watching him—I mean, her. She pulls back from the mule and wipes her eyes, then clears her throat and spits on the ground.

"I don't...I don't know what's wrong with me. It's just a mule." Old Nibs nuzzles her and puts his head on her shoulder. It's clear the mule is pretty shook up.

When Old Nibs does that, Lou's control slips again and new tears flow. She hugs the mule, quick and fierce. "It's just...Old Nibs has been with me for over seventeen years, longer than anyone in my family. Hell, he *is* my family."

She's trying hard to keep up the charade, but her voice keeps cracking. It goes from rough and gravelly to high-pitched and back again, all in a few seconds' time.

"It's okay, Lou," I say. "I know."

Lou gives me an odd look. "What?"

"I *know*. I know who you are. You don't have to pretend anymore."

"You know?" There goes the last of Lou's control. She wraps her arms around the mule's neck and begins sobbing. It goes on for quite a while and I get darned uncomfortable. I've always felt uncomfortable around women's tears and it's doubly hard to be around one I thought was a man until a couple minutes ago. Not knowing what else to do, I settle for patting her on the back.

Finally Lou pulls away from Old Nibs. The mule's shoulder is wet with tears. She gives him a last pat and goes and sits down by the fire. I do too.

"It's a relief, really," she says, wiping tears off her face. "Almost twenty-five years I've been pretending to be a man, and you're the first one to ever find me out. I guess I knew it had to happen eventually."

"How did it happen?" I know I'm not supposed to ask. This is the West. Half the people out here are running from something and the one unspoken rule is never to ask about their past. It's just not done. But I can't help myself.

Lou takes a deep breath. "It's a long story. I was raised in a fairly well-to-do family in Boston, given a good education, et cetera. When I turned eighteen my father announced that I would be marrying one of his business associates, a man twenty years older than me. I hated that man. His hands were always oily and the way he looked at me made me feel dirty.

"Also, I didn't want to marry. I saw where that led, popping out one baby after another until I was worn out and old before my time. I'd had years to watch my mother. I could see what a beautiful woman she'd been. I could see the real talent she had at the piano. And she could sing too, such a lovely voice. But she kept it all hidden. She lived in my father's shadow, like a flower kept in a dark room.

"I defied my father. I'd acted in some plays at finishing school and I told him I wanted to be an actress. He yelled at me, told me no daughter of his would be an actress, that it was little more than being a whore. He said I could marry or I could get out."

She stops, caught up in remembering. It's so strange for me to hear such a gentle voice coming from such a harsh looking person. It's not just the pitch of her voice that's changed, either. She speaks so differently. Gone is the rude, uneducated mule skinner and in his place is someone who sounds completely different.

"So I left. Ran away actually. I went to New York City. It was hard at first, but eventually I got a role in a play that did well and that led to other roles."

She looks up at the sky, lost in the past. "If only you could have seen me, up on the stage."

I cut in then. "A stage? You mean like a kind of wagon?"

She laughs. It sounds good on her. "Not that kind of stage."

She goes on to describe what a stage is and then I realize what she's talking about. "I know what a stage is. I've seen one before, but there was only one woman on it and she was dancing and taking off her clothes."

I trail off, feeling uncomfortable telling Lou about it. It was a strange experience. The men watching with me shouted and got very excited, but even though the woman took off quite a lot of clothing, by the end she was still wearing far more than the Apache women I'd grown up around. I left feeling like it was another example of the white man's world I didn't understand.

Lou shakes her head. "What you saw is called burlesque and it's not the same thing at all. I was an actress. The audiences loved me. They cried. They cheered. They threw roses on the stage. The critics said I was destined to be the next Sarah Bernhardt." She goes quiet, a little smile on her face, remembering.

I'm even more confused than before. "What did you do on stage that made people cry?"

She thinks I'm making fun of her. Her eyes narrow down and grumpy old mule-skinner Lou returns. Then she blinks and he goes away.

"My apologies, Ace. Of course you don't know about the theater, or Shakespeare, or any of that. How would you, after all?"

I don't say anything. Now I'm wondering what a shake spear is. Is it like a regular spear? Why would you shake it instead of throwing it?

"The stage is a place for acting out plays. Shakespeare was a man who lived a long time ago in England. He wrote lots of famous plays. Plays are like stories. Actors dress up in costumes and play different parts in those stories."

Well, that makes a little more sense. Not a lot, but a little. "You were an actor."

"An actress, actually. Bella Lucy, they called me. I was the most beautiful of them all."

I decide I'm still not getting this. "Why?"

Her smile fades. "What do you mean, 'why'?"

"Why do people do this, wander around on stage pretending to be someone they're not?"

"It's culture!" she cries, as if that explains anything at all, instead of confusing me further.

"Culture is…?"

"It is what separates us from the savages," she says, then grabs my arm. "No offense, my Indian friend."

I'm not offended, I'm confused. It seems there's no end to the crazy things white people do. "I still don't know what culture is."

"Culture is the arts. It is music. The theater. Painting. Sculpture." She sighs. "All the things we don't have out here in the West."

"I like paint," I say, thinking of the few painted houses I've seen. The General's hacienda, for instance, was painted a pleasant red color.

"Not paint. Paintings."

"Oh, paintings." I remember seeing those at the General's. "And a sculpture is…?"

"Something carved out of stone. A person usually."

"Oh." I remember those at the General's too. I remember thinking how useless they were. "So that is culture."

"Only part of it. There is literature too."

"Literature?"

"Stories, like theater, only written down instead of acted out."

"You mean books. I know what books are." I've seen a few, but I've never opened one.

"I've lost so much," she says, her voice cracking. "That's not true. I threw it away. I was so young and stupid. I was a star and now look at me! I'm driving a wagon in the middle of nowhere with a savage as my only companion." She wipes her eyes with the back of her hand. "No offense, Ace."

I'm not taking any. The things I've heard about the cities back East sound downright crazy to me. If that's culture, I'll take being a savage.

"Why did you leave?"

"I made a mistake," she sniffs. "A terrible, terrible mistake. It cost me everything. I've never told anyone, not a soul."

That sounds good to me, because I don't think I really want to hear about it. I'm having a hard time with this new Lou, hearing a woman's voice come out of that face. I'd rather go back to silence.

"But I can tell you, can't I, Ace? You'll listen to my story, won't you?"

I wince, but try not to let it show. "Sure. Tell me." I settle in. It's starting to seem like it's going to be a long night.

I should have just eaten the hog and hominy and kept my mouth shut.

14

"It was a love doomed to tragedy," she says. "Like all the great Greek tragedies, there was no way it wouldn't come to a bad end."

What's a Greek tragedy? I wonder. But I don't ask. I'm going to keep my questions to myself from now on. They only cause problems.

"I'd been on the stage for several years but I was still only a child when I met him. He was older than me by ten years, so handsome, so dashing. He was hired on at the theater where I worked and I fell in love with him immediately.

"I'd never been in love. Not really. I was completely unprepared for what happened to me. I never suspected how it would drive me crazy by the end. I should have seen what kind of man he was, that he was only toying with me. The signs were there even from the beginning, but I ignored them. I only saw what I wanted to see."

That gets my attention. I don't think I like where this is headed. It makes me think of Victoria. I should hate her, shouldn't I? How come I don't? Why do I have dreams where I hold her close and tell her everything is all right?

"What else could I do? I was caught up in the lights. Everything was perfect. We were in love and our future was golden."

She stops and wipes her eyes again. When she has herself together, she continues.

"Then *she* showed up. She was even younger than I was, with hair like spun gold, lips so full and red they were like ripe apples. It didn't take long before it started. I was blinded by love, but not so blind I couldn't see the way he looked at her, the way she laughed at everything he said.

"I tried desperately to stave off the inevitable. I threw myself at him. I did things for him, things no respectable young woman should ever do. But it did no good. Daily he drifted further from me. I became ill. I cried all the time and could hardly leave my room.

"It was when she got the lead role instead of me in our next play that I knew I had to act. I knew I had to get rid of her." Lou grabs my arm and gives me a pleading look. "You must understand. I was crazy, but not insane. I didn't want her to get hurt. I just wanted to humiliate her. I wanted him to see that she wasn't the one he wanted, but me.

"The set was supposed to collapse in the middle of her scene. I planned it all perfectly, I thought. I cut most of the way through the ropes holding it in place, figuring that when the stage hands pulled on them to lift them they would break, and the set would fall on her.

"Except that it didn't go that way. The scene came, she went out on stage, and every time they pulled on those ropes I waited for them to break and it all to come down on her. When nothing happened I remember thinking that maybe I cut the wrong ropes. There are so many of them backstage, and there's not much light so it's hard to see.

"Then my scene came. It was my favorite scene of the whole play. I got to sing this beautiful song while my former lover was drowning in the background."

That sounds crazy to me. What kind of woman sings while her lover is drowning?

She reads my expression. "I imagine that sounds awful, but it's opera and opera is like that. He had betrayed me with my best friend and so I arranged for him to drown, but at the same time I was filled with sorrow over his death. The song was my farewell to him. It was the last cry of my love, the outpouring of my sorrow.

"I was at the peak of the song, singing my heart out, when the ropes I cut finally gave way. I looked up as the set came down and the corner caught me right here." She points to her missing eye. "I was hoisted by my own petard."

"What's a petard?"

"It doesn't matter. What matters is that my life as I knew it was over. No one would hire a one-eyed actress. My beauty was gone. My career was gone. I went crazy then. I ran away and fled out west. I wanted to be invisible. I wanted to go where no one would ever notice me again."

"You never went back?"

"Never. I thought about it a few times, but I was too afraid. I wanted them to remember me as I was, not as I am."

We sit there in silence for a while. I want to get up and go set my snare, but I have this feeling there is something else Lou wants to say. Finally she looks at me shyly.

"Would you like to hear some? Some of my lines, I mean."

Why not? It's not going to make this night any stranger. I nod. Lou stands up and puts her hand to her throat. Seeing what looks like a gruff, crusty man standing there like a woman, I get that strange feeling again, like the world stopped making sense.

"'Thou knowest the mask of night is on my face, else would a maiden blush bepaint my cheek for that which thou hast heard me speak tonight. Fain would I dwell on form; fain, fain deny what I have spoke. But farewell compliment. Dost thou love me? I know thou wilt say 'Ay', and I will take thy word. Yet, if thou swear'st, thou mayst prove false.'"

She takes her hand away from her throat and looks at me. "Well?" she asks. "What do you think?"

I don't know what to think. I'm not even sure that was English I just heard. But Lou is looking at me with such sad eyes, and I think I have to give her something besides a dumb look. I'm lost until a sudden inspiration comes to me, something that happened at that burlesque show once the entertainment was over.

I start slapping my hands together, the same way I saw everyone else do in that tent. It seems just as ridiculous to me now as it did then, but it's apparently the right thing because Lou's sad eyes go away and a big smile crosses her face.

"Thank you. That means..." Her voice catches for a second and she has to clear her throat to continue. "That means a lot."

15

It's a couple days later and that thing Lou said to me about not talking back when she first hired me? Now I think she said it so she can do all the talking. Seriously. It's like twenty-five years of words built up and now the dam broke and they're flooding me out.

I spend a lot of time nodding and saying "okay" now. It's not so bad, really. She seems a lot happier. She smiles a lot more anyway. She calls me her 'savage friend' but I think she means it in a nice way so I don't mind much. She's like a young girl. I can't believe she's the same person at all.

We're up in the mountains now. The air is cool and there are pines and firs everywhere. We had a bear in our camp last night, but he was only poking around and he wandered off without any fuss.

One morning after we've been going for about an hour we get down in the bottom of this little ravine filled with aspens and rock outcroppings. We cross a little stream and then there's this creaking, cracking sound and a big aspen suddenly falls across the road in front of us.

The mules get all skittish, but before they can bolt Lou gets on top of them and gets them under control. I snatch up my Winchester.

I know what's coming.

"We got you surrounded and dead to rights! Drop your guns and no one gets hisself killed!"

Sure enough, there's a rifle barrel and the crown of a hat sticking over the top of the rock outcropping ahead to the right. There are shadowy figures back in the trees, a couple on each side.

"Be damned if I will! I've never lost a load to bandits and I don't aim to start now!" Lou yells back. All trace of the young girl is gone. It's crusty old Lou, the one-eyed mule skinner now. She's got old Betsy in hand. "You want my cargo you'll take it over my dead body."

So I guess I don't need to ask her how we're playing this. I wish she would've left off the part about dead bodies, though. I'm not all that keen on dying for some wooden boxes.

"Don't make it like that!" the man in the rocks yells. "You can walk on out of here. It ain't you we want!"

Lou cuts loose with a blue streak that would do any man in her trade proud. But I heard something. I put my hand on her arm. "Hold on."

She gives me a dark look, but the venom pouring out slows and stops. "Not getting cold feet, are you?" she hisses.

"I know that voice." To the man in the rocks I yell, "Is that you, Gimpy?"

A pause, then, "How'd you know my name? You cain't even see me!"

"I know your name because I know *you*." I push my hat back so they can all see my face clear.

"Is that you, Ace?"

Lou gives me a dead-eyed look. "You *know* these bandits? Did you set this up?" I think she's about a squirrel's twitch away from shooting me now. There's no way this is the woman I rode this wagon with for the last few days.

"Don't do anything hasty," I tell her in a low voice. "Especially don't shoot me. Let me talk to them."

I'm feeling a whole lot better about this now. Thinking I'm going to live through the day. The only thing that's got me worried is I haven't heard Boyce's voice yet. He's the one could make this all go to hell. He and I have a score to settle. "Why don't you come on out and let's talk, Gimpy."

Gimpy stands up. He's got a handkerchief pulled up over his face and his hat down low. "As I live and breathe, it *is* you, Ace. How come you ain't hanged?"

"It's a long story. How come you left me for the law?"

"Well, shoot, Ace. You know how Boyce is. I made a couple of noises, but I can't beat him and you know it."

"That's a damn lie, Gimpy!" one of the figures off to the right yells. "You didn't say a word. I was the only one to speak up."

"That you, Billy?" I call.

He comes forward out of the trees and pulls down the handkerchief covering his face. I see the little tuft of hair on his chin and the familiar straw hat with the narrow brim. "Good to see you ain't dead, Ace," he says.

"Dammit, Billy!" Gimpy yells. "What're you doing showing your face? This is a stick up. We're supposed to be ingoc…incognitos. We can't be incognitos if he knows who we are."

"Shut your yap, Gimpy! He already knows who we are and we know who he is. It's Ace."

Billy comes a little closer. He looks a little twitchy, probably on account of Lou has Betsy pointed square at his chest. "He ain't going to shoot me is he, Ace?"

"No, Billy." I put my hand on Betsy and push the barrel down.

"Dammit, Billy! You're doing it all wrong!" Gimpy yelps. "What's Boyce going to say?"

That makes me feel better, but I also feel disappointed. The last time I saw Boyce, he was hitting me over the head with a club and leaving me for the law. He almost got my neck stretched. I'd like to repay the debt with some lead interest.

"Where's Boyce?"

"Back to the hideout," Billy says. "His horse went down on him and he's stove up. He sent us out to watch this road and for some reason no one can figure, he put Gimpy in charge."

"That's right!" Gimpy yells. He's still up in the rocks. "I'm in charge! Don't you forget it."

"Where's Grady?" I ask.

Billy pushes his hat back and wipes his forehead. There's a lot of pimples on his forehead. He's still just a kid. "He cut out a couple days after Boyce whacked you. Said he wouldn't be part of no outfit that turned on its own like that."

"Grady was always a smart one. What are you still doing here?"

"Got nowhere else to go," Billy admits. "Thought of starting my own gang, but who'd join up?" He gets a sudden idea. I can see it on his face. Billy's not what you call subtle. "What about you, Ace? You want to start a gang?" The idea excites him and as often happens when he gets excited, his voice cracks a little.

"What about it, Ace?" Lou echoes.

I ignore her and stay focused on Billy. "I've gone straight, Billy. Almost getting hung was enough to convince me."

"Oh," Billy says, his smile fading. "I can see that might put a damper on things."

"If I was going to join a gang with someone, Billy, it'd be you. You know that, right?"

Billy's smile comes back. He strikes me as someone who never had that big brother he needed so bad.

"Well, consarn it, if you two are just gonna keep up with your little tea chat, then I'm coming down. I'm tired of sitting up in these rocks." Gimpy starts making his way down through the rocks.

16

The others come on out then too. The first one to emerge is wearing a shapeless mess of sweat-stained hat. One of his eyes doesn't point in the right direction.

"Howdy, Slow Eye," I say.

"Howdy, Ace," he mumbles.

The next one is tall and skinny with a dour look on his pinched up face. He's still pointing his rifle at me.

"Always a pleasure, Wilson," I say.

"So you say."

"Just point the rifle down already," Billy says.

The last one to emerge trips over a fallen tree limb and when he hits the ground his gun goes off. The others swear at him. He stands up. "It coulda happened to anybody," he says sullenly.

"Glad to see Boyce hasn't shot you yet, Timmons," I say. Boyce almost shot Timmons when he dropped our dynamite in the water.

"Not yet, but he keeps threatening."

"Just so you know," Slow Eye says to me, "I'm glad we don't have to shoot you. You don't seem like such a bad feller."

"Boyce ain't going to be happy about this," Wilson says. He's not exactly pointing his rifle at me, but he's still holding it like he might any second.

"We don't have to tell him, do we?" Slow Eye says. "We could say it was some other man, someone we didn't know, who was riding shot gun. S'long as we have the freight, he won't care about the details."

I feel Lou go tense beside me. The shotgun is still cocked. Slow Eye doesn't realize how close he is to getting a large hole in his chest.

"You're not taking the freight," I tell him.

"Goddammit, Ace!" Gimpy yells. He slipped coming down out of the rocks and has a scrape on the side of his face. "Why didn't you say so when I was still back in the rocks? Now it's going to get messy."

"You didn't ask."

"We dropped a tree on you. We're wearing hankies on our faces! What did you think we was here for?"

"I thought maybe you showed up to explain why you left me to the law."

All of them choose that moment to look somewhere else. Not a one of them will meet my eye.

"There wasn't much we could do," Slow Eye says. "Not with the law coming and Boyce on the prod."

"About that cargo…" Gimpy says.

"You're not taking it and that's that. You don't want me to shoot all of you, do you?"

That makes them go quiet. They've seen me shoot.

"Now, Ace, be reasonable," Gimpy says. "We can't show up back at the hideout empty-handed. You know how Boyce is."

"Go on back and tell him what I said, then. Tell him I'll face him one-on-one any time he wants."

"I ain't doing that. He'll shoot me."

"And I'll shoot you if you try to take this freight. I took a job to protect it and I aim to do that."

Wilson's expression gets even sourer than it was. "I wish you wouldn't have said that. Now we have to up and kill you. It spoils the mood."

But now Billy swings toward Wilson. "If you shoot Ace, I'm fixing to shoot you."

"Shut up. You ain't nothing but a wet-behind-the-ears kid, Billy."

"I'm a kid what can kill you," Billy replies in a low, dangerous voice. That's the voice he gets right before he starts spraying lead everywhere.

"You all shut the hell up!" Gimpy explodes. "Boyce put me in charge. Me. No one's shooting anyone without my say-so."

"I'm getting sick of hearing you go on about that," Wilson says to Gimpy. "Ever since we left the hideout you've done nothing but squawk about how Boyce put you in charge. You wouldn't be in charge if I put a bullet in your gut."

Slow Eye has a confused look on his face. He's swinging his gun from me, to Billy, to Wilson. "What's going on here?" he cries. "If the shooting starts, who'm I supposed to shoot?"

"No one's shooting anyone," Lou suddenly says.

"No one asked you!" Gimpy hollers. "Don't confuse the issue more."

"I'm not confusing it. I'm about to make it real clear for you." She hooks a thumb at the back of the wagon. "You boys have any idea who I'm hauling this for? Do you know whose name is on this freight you're so hot to get your hands on?"

General shrugs all around. "What difference does it make?" Gimpy says. "We're outlaws. We don't care if it belongs to the President hisself."

"Are you sure about that?"

Something in her tone gets through to all of them. I admit to being a bit anxious to know myself.

"You ever hear of Dace Jackson?" she asks.

Everyone goes dead quiet. Of course they've heard of Dace. Everyone who isn't dead has heard of Dace. He's only the owner of the biggest spread in the Arizona Territory.

"That belongs to Dace?" Timmons asks in a shaky voice.

"It does." Lou pauses to let that sink in. "Do you know what Dace will do if he doesn't get it?"

Slow Eye lowers his gun. Wilson pales and takes a step back. Gimpy looks sick.

"I don't want to know," Timmons says in a shaky voice. He looks at the others. "I vote we let this wagon go."

"I agree," Slow Eye says quickly. "I never even seen it."

"We were never here," Timmons adds, putting his pistol away.

The only one who still looks undecided is Gimpy. "Boyce put me in charge," he moans. "If I come back with nothing, he ain't ever going to trust me again."

"He don't trust you anyway," Billy pipes up. "So that won't change."

Gimpy glares at him.

"What's he going to say if you show up and a couple dozen of Dace's men come tagging along?" I ask him. "Have you thought about that?"

"God bless it!" Gimpy snaps. "Don't anything ever go right with this gang? Back down, boys. Put your guns away."

I don't bother to point out that everyone has already done that. Leave the man something for his pride, I say.

"It was good to see you again, Ace," Billy says.

"Likewise," Slow Eye adds. "I'm glad I didn't have to shoot you."

"And I'm glad I didn't have to shoot you first," I say.

"So all this effort was for nothing?" Wilson says. I know how lazy he is, how much he hates effort. "Shouldn't we at least rob the two of them? Why would Dace care about that?"

"You'd get nothing from me," I tell him. "Why do you think I'm riding this job? I'm broke."

"We could still take your pistols. And your horse," he says sullenly.

"You know what would happen if you tried to take my guns," I tell him. "And worse would happen if you tried to take Coyote. You know he has a special hatred for you." It's true. Coyote bit a chunk out of his shoulder once.

"And Betsy here would cut you in half before you laid a hand on me," Lou says.

"All right then," Wilson grouses. "You can stop with the threats. I get the idea."

They start to head for their horses, but Lou stops them. "Ain't you forgetting something?"

"Yeah, we're forgetting that we're outlaws," Wilson says.

"Not that." She points at the tree across the road. "That."

17

"Are we really delivering this freight to Dace Jackson?" I ask Lou once we're under way again.

"Yup."

That gives me something to think about. Dace Jackson owns the Hashknife Ranch, two thousand square miles of land stretching halfway across the Territory. Word is he has lunch with the President when he goes to Washington, D.C. So, yeah, he's what you'd call a big deal. Definitely not someone you want to cross.

"You used to run with those low-lifes?"

"For a spell."

Lou grunts. I can tell she's upset with me.

"I had a bit of trouble in Texas a while back. There wasn't much work after that. But I was telling the truth. I've gone straight since then."

Lou gives me a long look, then says, "I guess I'm not one to pass judgment when a man ain't all he appears to be."

"Does this mean you'll keep reciting those scenes for me?" I ask.

Lou's answer is a girlish smile and just like that the female Lou is back. I'm glad to see her. I have to admit, I like this woman. She's made this trip go a whole lot easier, acting out pieces of the plays she's been in. I don't understand all of it, but the words ring fine on my ear anyhow.

Things stay pretty quiet the next few days while we travel through the mountains. It's fine country, lots of grassy meadows, streams with trout in them, high peaks waiting for the winter snows. Finally we come through a pass and look down on a wide, grassy valley with a big house and a mess of corrals and barns and buildings in the middle. Dace's spread.

We head down the slope. Coyote's staying close, which I'm glad to see. I don't want any of Dace's hands thinking he's a stray and dropping a rope on him.

"What do you think is in those crates?" I ask Lou.

"I don't. I learned a long time ago to do my job and leave it at that."

"Not even a little bit curious?"

"Curiosity killed the cat."

That stumps me. I've never heard that before. "What cat?"

She gives me a look to see if I'm toying with her. "It's not a particular cat. Just a general cat."

"How would curiosity kill a cat? I don't understand."

"It's just a saying, Ace. Leave it at that."

I have to admit, it's an impressive spread. The house is huge and looks like it sprawls over a couple of acres. There are four separate buildings besides the house and about twenty corrals. I count a couple dozen cowboys and a handful of general working folk scurrying around like they all have somewhere they had to be yesterday.

Lou calls out to one who's passing by. "I've got a delivery here. The name on the slip is Buford. Where do I find him?"

The man points to one of the buildings. "You'll find the foreman over there."

The building looks like some kind of blacksmith's shop. There's smoke coming out the chimney and the sound of hammers banging on metal. A door opens as we roll up and a man comes out. He's stripped to the waist and sooty-looking. Probably not the foreman.

"Is Buford in there?" Lou asks him, shouting to be heard over the din. That woman can shout like a man, that's for sure.

The man closes the door. It's a lot easier to hear now. "He's in the back." Then he just stands there, picking at something in his ear.

"Well?"

"Well, what?"

"Don't stand there. Go get him."

"Like hell I will," the man says. "You can fetch him yourself. Or have your damned Injun fetch him for you." He adds a rude gesture to make sure we got the message.

Quick as a snake's tongue that bullwhip flashes out and the tip lays a stripe across his hand. He yelps and draws it back,

"What did ya go and do that for?"

"Keep a civil tongue in your head. He's not my Indian."

"Coulda just said so. You didn't have to whip me."

"You'll remember longer this way. Now are you fetching Buford or do I gotta whip you again?"

"I'm going." He goes back inside, sucking on his injured hand.

Buford comes out a minute later. He's a big man, wide across the shoulders and an ample gut that isn't all fat. He's got thick jowls and his eyes are all but lost behind heavy eyelids. He's all duded up in a white suit with a string tie.

But it's not him I'm looking at. It's the man next to him.

With a growl, I reach for my gun.

18

Lou grabs my wrist in an iron grip. "Roll it back, cowboy," she hisses.

I nod and let go of my gun. Lou's right. Now is a bad time. Fortunately, the men were talking to each other as they came out the door and neither one saw what I did.

"And stay down," Lou adds in a low voice. "We don't want any trouble here."

It goes against all my instincts, but I pull my hat down and try my best to be invisible.

Buford looks up at us. "You have something for me?" he rumbles.

From under the brim of my hat I watch the man next to him. It's Wilkins, the man who accused me of cattle rustling back when I was a hand on the Bar T ranch in Texas. He's a short man, with a sallow, pock-marked face and a thin, little ferret mouth.

Wilkins looks right at me, but he doesn't see me. That's fine with me. I want him surprised when I pop up with some payback.

Lou pulls some folded sheets of paper out of her inside pocket and holds them up. "My orders were to deliver these crates to James Buford and no one else. Are you him?"

Buford jerks his head and Wilkins scurries up and takes the papers from Lou. Up close I hate him even more. He might just have the most punchable face I've ever seen.

Wilkins gives the papers to Buford, who looks them over. When he looks up again he's a lot more interested than before. He comes over and looks in the wagon bed, runs his hands over the crates. "I wasn't expecting you for a few days yet. You made good time."

"I don't believe in dilly-dallying," Lou says.

"Get some boys and get these crates unloaded right away," Buford says to Wilkins. "Mind you be careful with them, you hear?"

"Got it, boss," Wilkins says and hurries off.

Buford stuffs the papers in his pocket and starts to walk off, but Lou calls out to him. "I need to get paid."

Buford turns back, looking irritated at her tone. He takes a scrap of paper from another pocket and scrawls on it with a stub of pencil. "Take this over to the office. The man working the desk will get you paid."

A big sliding door opens and a half dozen men come out, all of them stripped down and sooty like the first one. Wilkins is with them and under his direction they unload the crates and haul them inside. Wilkins stands by the door while they work, his thumbs hooked in his belt. He looks over at me and I dip my head a little so he can't get a good look at my face. He frowns like a man on the verge of remembering something and I let my hand drift near my gun again.

But he doesn't say anything and a few minutes later we're on our way to the office.

"What's got you all hot and bothered?" Lou asks.

"The little guy. I used to work with him on a ranch in Texas."

"I take it it didn't end well."

"He accused me of rustling. Got them all riled up for a lynching party in my honor."

"And now you're bent on revenge."

"You could call it that. I'd call it justice."

"Were you really going to shoot him right there? With all these men around?"

"I don't know. Maybe I just would've winged him."

"You men are all the same. Act now, think later."

"Said by the woman with one eye."

She nods and spits. "Point taken."

We pull up to the office and get down off the wagon. Inside, behind the desk, is a man in a vest and white shirt, wearing an eye shade. He's chewing on an unlit cigar. He looks up and scowls at us.

Lou tosses the scrap of paper down on his desk and he squints at it. "Money, is it?" he asks. "That's what you're here for?"

Lou nods.

The man gets up and goes to a large safe against the wall, muttering to himself as he goes. "Not so much as a 'Hello,

69

Howard,' or a 'Fine day isn't it, Howard.' It's nothing but money, money, money. Nothing else matters."

"We can hear you," Lou says.

He looks over his shoulder from where he's kneeling in front of the safe. "You can? The Lord be blessed."

He gets the money out and comes back to the desk. "How were we supposed to know your name is Howard?" I ask.

He points. There's a block of wood on his desk with his name on it.

He counts out the money and hands it over to Lou. "Much obliged, Howard," I say, touching the brim of my hat.

Howard nods. "A little civility don't cost much, does it?"

We climb back on the wagon. I hate this wagon. I can't wait to get back on Coyote. Lou picks up the reins and her whip. A man comes up to us and puts his hand on the brake. He's wearing a long apron with blood stains on it. In one hand he's got a meat cleaver.

"Is that the horse?" he asks, nodding at Coyote. "How come he's got no halter on him?"

"What're you talking about?" I say.

"It's a simple question. Is that the horse? The dogs are hungry."

I look over his shoulder, back toward the main house. There's a kennel there, with a dozen hounds in it. They're all watching the man closely. Hungrily.

"C'mon. I got lots of other things to do. Put a halter on that nag and lead him over here."

"Easy, Ace," Lou warns, seeing my hand drift close to my pistol.

"Are you thinking about feeding Coyote to those dogs? Is that it?" I say in a low voice.

"What did you think I was saying? Mr. Jackson, he wants his dogs fed on fresh meat. Usually it's beef, but they have a special taste for horse meat." He hefts the cleaver and takes a step toward Coyote. "Let's get this over with."

Now my gun is out. "If you touch that horse, I'll shoot you in places you didn't know you had."

He takes a step back, putting up his hands. "Easy there, pardner. I had no idea you were so attached to that crowbait."

"*Crowbait*? Did you just call Coyote crowbait?"

"Ace, could we just leave here without you shooting someone?" Lou says.

"I guess we'll see," I reply. "It depends on him."

The man has turned pale. "I don't want no trouble. I'm just doing my job. I'm sorry."

"Apologize."

"What? I just did."

"Not to me. To him." I point at Coyote, who is watching the whole thing closely, like he knows it's about him.

The man turns to Coyote. "I'm...sorry?"

"Take off your hat. And say it like you mean it."

The man takes his hat off. His hair is greasy and stuck to his head. "I'm sorry." He looks back at me. "Is that good?"

"It will do," I say, putting my pistol away. The man all but runs away.

"Really, Ace?" Lou says. "It's just a horse."

I waggle a finger at her. "Coyote is *not* just a horse."

Lou sighs. "Can we leave now? Or is there someone else here you want to shoot first?"

"I want to shoot Buford. I don't like the looks of that man."

"Maybe later, okay?"

"Okay." I put my pistol away. "Maybe later."

We roll on out of there and when we're a good distance away, she stops. She counts out a few bills and gives them to me.

"Thanks, Lou. This is more than I expected."

She grunts, very much the crusty old mule-skinner Lou. "You earned it. Call it hazard pay."

"Facing down my old gang?"

"No." Lou winks at me. "Listening to me. It can't have been easy." It's young, girlish Lou again.

"That's amazing how you do that, you know," I say. "You're a hell of an actress. I don't have anyone to compare you to, but I don't think there's any better than you."

She does a little bow there on the seat. I get down and pull my saddle out of the back of the wagon, start saddling Coyote.

71

"What're you going to do now?" I ask her.

She holds up the rest of the bills. "There's a little town, not too far from here, name of Lily Creek. I'm going to go over there and see if I can spend a little of this money. I'm sick of eating my own cooking and a bed wouldn't be too bad."

"Lily Creek? Sounds like a nice place. A whole lot nicer than Tombstone."

"If you happen to end up there too, I might see my way to buying you a dinner."

"Really? What will people say, if they see crusty, old, one-eyed Lou buying food for a no-account, half-breed Injun?"

"They'll say I went soft in the head."

"I won't pass that up," I say, tightening the cinch and dodging Coyote's bite. "But I'm not sitting on that wagon seat for another mile. I'm going to have splinters in my ass until I'm an old man."

19

Lily Creek *is* a nice town. So nice that I'm suspicious. I'm used to flea-bitten cow towns and hardscrabble mining towns. But Lily Creek is different.

For one thing, there aren't any saloons. At least, none that I can see. For another, there's no boot hill. Sure, there's a graveyard, but it's a small one, over behind the church. And it's a real church, painted white, with a steeple and a bell and everything.

The houses and shops are laid out in neat lines. And they don't look like a drunk cowboy built them in an afternoon. They look built to last, nice and solid and square. The homes all have big gardens out back, busting with vegetables at this time of the year, and most have little white fences around the front, big, bright sunflowers heavy with seeds hanging over them.

It's easily the prettiest town I've ever seen. It looks like people who plan on staying there and raising kids, which isn't the case with most towns out here in the West. To top it off, it's set in a pretty little valley nestled up in the mountains. There's a feisty little stream running through town, lots of big, green, grassy meadows and little patches of aspens and firs here and there.

There's even kids, running around chasing each other and screeching like banshees.

Not a bad little place at all.

"Wow," Lou says.

"Good word."

We've pulled up at the edge of town and we're taking it all in.

"I didn't know there were places like this," she says. "Not out here."

I suddenly realize how dirty and disreputable I am. I try spitting on my fingers and rubbing out a few of the worst stains on my shirt, but it's basically hopeless. "Let's just try and not frighten them, okay?"

"Says the man who looks like a bloodthirsty Apache," she replies with a grin.

"I don't look bloodthirsty. Just thirsty. For water. Or maybe whiskey."

"You're not going to shoot anybody, are you?"

"Not right away, anyway."

We head on into town. The whole way I'm telling myself this place can't be as sweet as it looks. I've just been out in the wilderness for too long.

But I'm wrong. It really is that nice.

Right after we get into town there's this little girl with black hair walking down the street, holding a bunch of wildflowers in her hand. She's a little thing, not much more than a wisp, and she runs right up to my horse, which makes me a little tense. Coyote hates all people pretty much equally. It's not past him to bite this poor girl's arm off.

But Coyote does nothing and she holds up a flower to me. I bend down out of the saddle and take it from her.

"What's this for?"

"You look grumpy," she says, in what must be the cutest little voice ever. "Flowers help me when I'm grumpy."

I take the flower and wonder if I really look grumpy. Maybe I ought to try smiling more.

"Thanks," I tell the little girl and stick the flower in my hair. Long hair is good for some things.

She giggles and runs off down the street.

"Don't you look adorable," Lou says.

"You promised me dinner," I say gruffly. "Don't think of backing out now."

We ride on down the street. Now, I've been in quite a few towns in my time since leaving my clan. I'm used to the suspicious looks from most of the menfolk, the half-fearful looks from the women. I'm used to hostility and veiled threats. But there's none of that here. Men and women both smile openly and nod their welcome.

I don't quite know how to act.

"What's going on here?" I whisper to Lou.

"It's called hospitality. Just enjoy it, Ace."

We pull up to the livery and put the mules and Coyote into the corral. The man who comes out to greet us has a full beard that wraps around his chin and clear up into his hair, but he has no mustache. He's wearing a hat with a round brim and a round crown. When he smiles, his whole face crinkles up.

"Welcome to Lily Creek, strangers. I'm Lucas."

Lou holds out some money to him, but he puts his hands up. "You don't need to do that. Just pay when you leave."

I stare at him and try to keep my mouth from dropping open.

"Thank you, Lucas," Lou says. "My name's Lou and this here is Ace." She's still talking like a man, but her voice is noticeably softer.

"You'll be looking for a bed and a meal," Lucas says. He points. "Right on over there is Pearl's place. She runs the best boarding house in town. It's also the only boarding house." He laughs, a friendly sound that comes from way down in his belly. I get the feeling I might like this place.

We head on over toward the boarding house and Lou says, "So, what do you think of Lily Creek so far?"

Before I can respond, gunshots fill the air and a whole pack of cowboys comes racing into town, waving their guns around.

20

They're at the far end of the street, four of them on horseback, whooping it up and firing into the air.

Down near them is two-horse buggy, with a man just climbing into the seat. At the sound of the gunshots, the horses bolt. The man loses his hold and tumbles off the wagon into the street.

Horses and buggy come racing our way. I hear Lou curse and turn to see what she's cursing at.

The little girl is standing frozen in the middle of the street, staring at the oncoming buggy, her eyes wide.

Lou's already moving. I take off after her and pass her. I realize quick I'm not going to make it. The horses are too close and I'm not fast enough. But Lou, now a couple steps behind me, pulls up.

I hear a hiss and the whip snaps past my ear, popping one of the horses on the neck and causing it to veer sideways, banging into the other horse. That slows the buggy just enough that I'm able to get to the girl and scoop her up. One of the horses hits me with its shoulder as they fly by, knocking me down. I roll, shielding the girl in my arms.

I get to my feet and look at her. "Are you okay?"

She nods at me mutely, her eyes huge in her little face.

I carry her over to the side of the street and set her down. "Stay here, okay?"

I head for the four idiots on the horses. At least they're not shooting their guns anymore, but I see they've surrounded a young woman on foot and they're yelling things at her. Things that shouldn't be said to a lady.

Now I'm mad. Bad enough they almost got that child hurt. But now they're harassing a woman.

Not while I'm in town.

I hot foot it down there. On the way I pass by the sheriff's office and I see him standing out front, staring at the goings on.

His hand is on his gun butt, but he's not moving. He looks like he's about to run back inside and bolt the door.

The woman they're harassing is wearing a calico dress and a bonnet. The four cowboys are circling around her on their horses, cutting her off every time she tries to get away.

One of them, with long, red hair and a blotchy face calls out. "Where ya going, darlin'? We just want to talk to you."

The others hoot at this and one of them yells, "Sure, we just want to talk!"

The young woman sees an opening and tries to run for it, but the red-haired one leans down out of his saddle and snatches her arm roughly. "Don't you know it's rude to run off like that?" He jerks on her arm when he says it and she cries out a little.

I don't remember drawing them, but both my Colts are in my hands suddenly. I point and shoot all in the same motion and red hair's hat goes flying off.

"Take your hands off her," I say. I could add a threat, but I think the flying hat and the two Colts does a good enough job that I don't need to add anything.

All four look at me. Red-hair's still got a hold of the woman and the edges of his mouth draw down.

"This don't concern you, Injun!" he snarls. "Walk away or we'll gun you down right here."

"Don't you know who we are, you damned fool?" another yells. "Why, we—"

I've heard all I need to hear. All of them have pistols out and a couple are already pointing at me. I don't see the point in a lot of jawing when we all know how this is going to go.

The first shot takes red-hair in the forearm so he squawks and lets go of the woman. Look at that. I told him to let go of her and he did. All it took was a little persuasion.

One of the others cusses and swings his pistol toward me. I could shoot him right between the eyes, but I'm still hoping we can get out of this without too much mess. I'm a stranger around here and it would probably be best if I could avoid killing anyone for a day or two. At least until I suss the lay of the land.

So I shoot the pistol out of his hand. There's a clang of lead on steel. The gun goes flying and he screams, a high, girlish sound. "My damn hand!" he howls. "He shot my damn hand!"

Shut up, you baby. I shot your gun, not your hand.

The third one shoots at me, but his horse isn't liking all this gunfire and is hopping around and the shot goes wild. I decide to egg his horse on a bit and put a couple rounds in the dirt between his legs. Now the horse is definitely unhappy about the current events and so he just up and bucks his rider right off and races off out of town, reins flapping behind him.

I turn to the fourth one and realize I made a serious mistake. I wasn't paying him enough attention because I didn't think he had his gun out, but now I see it was hidden down by his leg. Lots of men panic when lead starts flying and you can count on them to miss, but the way he brings the gun around real steady and points it at my chest makes me think he isn't going to miss.

I'm trying to get my gun up, knowing I'm too late, when something wraps around his wrist. His pistol belches flame, but the shot goes high and wild as his arm is pulled hard to the side.

It's Lou. She's got that bullwhip wrapped around his forearm and before he can recover, she gives it another, harder yank, backed up by muscles built up from years of mule-skinning.

With a surprised yelp, he tumbles clean out of the saddle and hits the ground hard. He gets up and tries for his gun, which he lost on the way down, but the bullwhip snaps again and he falls back, holding a bloody stripe on his cheek.

"The next one takes off your ear," she says. He stops going for his gun.

Red-hair is still holding his bleeding forearm. "You just made the biggest mistake of your life," he tells me.

I make a show of looking around. They're all bleeding. The one who got bucked off isn't moving. The one who got the gun shot out of his hand is cradling it to his chest and crying, snot running down his face. "I think you're confused about who made the mistake."

"You have any idea who we are?"

"The four dumbest pilgrims to ever draw on a pair of boots?"

"We're from the Hashknife ranch. You know what that means?"

"I don't, but I guess you're going to tell me."

"It means you're dead. You and your ugly, one-eyed friend there."

Lou makes it look so casual, so easy. She barely moves her arm at all, but that bullwhip snaps out and takes a piece of red-hair's ear right off.

Oops. I could have told him that was a bad idea. But then, he didn't ask.

"What the hell?" he screams. "That *hurt*!"

"I believe that was the general idea," I tell him.

"Now you're really in trouble!" he yells.

"You said that already. Say something new."

"I don't believe he's got anything new to say," Lou says, and spits on the ground.

"Why don't you and your friends pack up and leave?" I suggest. "Before my friend there decides to remove one of your eyes."

Lou pops her whip so the tip snaps right near his face. His eyes bug out in his head.

"He has a collection of them, you know," I tell him. "Always trying to replace the one he lost."

It takes them a few minutes, but they finally get loaded up— the unconscious one strapped across the back of red-hair's saddle—and leave. Red-hair is still snarling threats, but I made them leave all their guns in the dirt so there's no point in listening to them.

"The Hashknife ain't done with you yet, not by a long shot!" He raises his voice to shout at the townsfolk who've gathered at a safe distance to watch. "You hear me? This changes nothing! You take Dace's offer or we're coming back and wipe this town clean off the earth!"

21

"Thank you, Mr...."

It's the young woman we saved from the riders.

"No mister. It's just Ace. And this is Lou," I say.

"I'm Annie," she says.

"What's going on here?" Lou asks. "What was all that business about taking offers?"

"Dace Jackson has been trying to buy us out since early summer. All along we've been saying no. Last week he sent that animal Buford over along with a couple dozen of his thugs. He told us we had two weeks to take his final offer, fifty dollars a lot. He said if we didn't take it, we'd all regret it."

There must be twenty townsfolk gathered around us by now and there's lots of nodding heads.

"It's not enough," one man says. He's wearing the heavy leather apron of a blacksmith and he has black hair and thunderous scowl. "Our land's worth four times that, easy."

"And we don't want to leave," an old woman adds. She's a tiny thing, with white hair and gnarled hands. Her eyes are sharp though. They look like the eyes of someone who doesn't miss much. "This is our home."

More nodding and agreeing. The crowd parts then and the sheriff comes up. He's a tall man, with a hangdog face and tiny little ears. "Why'd you have to go and do that?" he asks us. "Now you gone and got them all riled up."

"We got *them* riled up?" I can't believe what I'm hearing.

"They weren't going to hurt nothing," he says. "They were just kicking up their heels. They're scalawags, but that's it. If you'd done nothing, they would have gone on their way after a bit."

"Not going to hurt anything? Did you miss the part where the little girl almost got run down by the buggy?" Lou asks. She looks like she wants to use the whip on him.

"I'm okay!" a small voice yells. Sure enough, there's the little girl, pushing her way through the townsfolk. She trots over and grabs my hand. "I gave him a flower!" she cries. "See it in his hair?"

Annie whisks her off her feet and squeezes her tight. "I was so worried, Camila," she murmurs.

"It's okay, Mama. My new friend saved me."

The sheriff says, "It was an accident. Old Brady should have better control of his horses. And he should have set his brake. I've told him time and again if he didn't set it there was going to be an accident someday. Those horses are too green and prone to spooking."

I exchange a look with Lou. My look says, Are you hearing what I'm hearing? I can see she feels the same way.

"Seems to me you're not real clear about what it means to be the sheriff," I tell him.

"Is that what you think?" He walks up to me real close and looks down on me. He's taller than I am. "You know what I think?"

Honestly? No idea. I sure don't expect what comes next.

"I think you're right. You know what else?" He takes off his badge and turns to face the crowd. "I quit! You hear me? I quit! I didn't sign on for this shit. Look at me. My hair's done turned gray and it's starting to fall out. I took this job because I thought it would be easy. Hell, it was easy. Nothing ever happens in Lily Creek. No gunfights. No hangings. You don't even have a proper saloon!"

He turns back to me and hands me the star. "Here you go, amigo. I hope you enjoy your new career in law enforcement." He turns and stomps off. "I'm out of here. Good luck not dying!"

I stand there holding the star, a whole lot of things going through my head. Mostly they're of the how-the-shit-did-this-just-happen variety. Aren't I still a wanted man in Colorado? Probably Texas too?

I look up at the townsfolk. "I think there's been a mistake."

"You're darned right there has been," Annie says. She steps up to me and snatches the star from my hand. Up close I can see how amazingly green her eyes are.

She turns to the others. "I say the mistake was made when we hired old Tom to be our sheriff. Who here thinks Ace should be our new sheriff?"

There's a pause, while people look at each other. I'm expecting them to shake their heads, maybe even start laughing. I mean, who hires a drifter half-breed to be their sheriff?

But to my surprise they're doing neither. Most of them are actually nodding, as if what Annie said makes sense. Is this town crazy?

"Maybe we should talk about this a bit," I say. "I've never been a sheriff before. I don't even really know what's going on."

"The stranger is right about one thing," a new voice says. It's a heavyset man with thick, sagging cheeks. He's wearing a black top hat and black suit, with a little gold chain running across his large stomach. I'm willing to bet my pistols he's the banker in this town. Bankers have a look about them. I instinctively don't like him.

"With all deference to Miss Annie, we need to talk about this some more." He touches the brim of his hat and gives a little bow toward her as he says this. I don't miss the way her lip curls. "This is a big decision, and not one that should be made lightly. What do we know about this stranger anyway? How do we know he isn't an outlaw?"

That last part makes me flinch a little. Too close to home.

"He just saved my little girl, Herm," Annie says defiantly. "And he saved me too, in case you missed that part. He put himself at risk to do that, without knowing me, without knowing a one of us in this town. I don't need to know more than that."

"Maybe that's enough for you, Miss Annie," Herm continues, "but some of us are a little more sober-minded than you, not quite as...uh, how shall I put it? Not quite as high strung and prone to flights of excitement as you are."

The smug smile he gives her when he's done makes me want to punch him in the stomach. Annie looks like she wants to also.

"Is that all?" she says sarcastically. "Don't you want to pat me on the head when you say that?"

"Now, Miss Annie. You've had a scare and you're upset. It's making you hear things I never intended to say."

A little boy, probably about a year younger than Camila, makes his way through the crowd right then. Calling "Mama!" he runs to Annie and grabs onto her leg. She picks him up and sets him on her other hip.

"Here's what I propose, folks," Herm says, turning to the gathered townsfolk. "Let's gather everyone at the church and discuss this like adults. Say, in about an hour? That will give everyone time to cool down, allow reason to prevail over emotion. How does that sound?"

A minute later it's decided and people drift off until it's just me, Lou, Herm, Annie and the children. Holding the children's hands, Annie comes over to me.

"Thank you again, Ace. I'll see you at the church, won't I?"

With her looking at me like that, how could I say no? "I'll be there." She gives me a smile that makes my heart flip over and leads the children away.

Then Herm comes up. He gives me a look that says it's time for the adults to talk seriously. My dislike for him gets stronger.

"Don't get me wrong, stranger. We're grateful for you've done here today." Funny thing is, he doesn't sound grateful. He sounds oily, like he's selling something I don't want to buy. "In fact, I'd like to buy you both dinner and a bed for the night at Pearl's boarding house, just to show my thanks. How does that sound?"

When I don't respond, his confidence seems to waver a bit and he frowns.

"But you should understand one thing." He leans in closer. I can smell some kind of flowery scent coming off him. But it's too strong. "You will never be our sheriff. I will see to it, I promise you. What you will do is take your free meal and your free bed and in the morning you and your unsavory friend will ride away from Lily Creek and never come back."

"How about this instead?" I say. "You give up on this foolish notion that you can run me or Lou out of this town. I don't know how long you've been getting away with running roughshod over the people here, but I promise you it won't work with us."

The flesh around his eyes tightens. "Be careful you do not make an enemy of me, drifter. I have powerful friends. You will regret it."

As he's walking away I call after him. "Does this mean we don't get our free meal?"

22

"What was that all about?" Lou asks me after the banker is gone.

"Someone's got something to hide. That's what I think."

Lou spits on the ground and wipes her lip. "I don't know about you, but that makes me want to stick around for a couple of days."

"I feel the same way. Want to head on over to Pearl's, see if we can get something to eat before this meeting at the church?"

She squints at me. "By god, you're thinking about doing it, ain't you?"

"It can't hurt to hear them out. Besides, I need a job."

"You weren't too bad riding shotgun. We didn't get killed anyhow. Maybe I can use you for another run."

"I don't know, Lou. It's a good offer, but it sounds to me like these people could really use my help here."

She makes a disgusted sound.

"What's that for?"

"This ain't about needing a job. It ain't about helping these poor townsfolk, neither," she says.

"Okay, Lou. Then tell me what it's about."

"It's about that purty little thing and her green eyes. That's what."

"She has green eyes?"

"Horse shit," she growls. "Don't act like you didn't notice. You don't have the chops. She batted her eyelashes at you and now you're all hot to throw away your life on some impossible mission. You men are all the same."

"Okay, so maybe her eyes had something to do with it. But it's not the only reason."

Lou snorts again.

"Is it just me you have a low opinion of, or is it all men?" I ask her.

"I've had twenty years of studying you all up close. Trust me, it's *all* men." She pulls out her block of tobacco and bites off another piece.

"Susannah, the girl from the theater, who stole my man?" she says in a low voice. "Over the years I've come to see she did me a favor. If it wasn't for her, I might have married that idiot."

"You're a real romantic, Lou. You know that?"

Lou grunts and spits.

Pearl's boarding house is nothing like the one I stayed in back in Tombstone. It's clean, for one thing. There's lacy curtains on the windows and flowers in vases on the tables. The place smells like fresh bread, which makes my stomach wake up and grumble.

Pearl comes bustling out of the kitchen, wiping her hands on her apron. She's a tall, strong-looking woman with curly red hair and long earrings that tinkle when she walks.

"Welcome to Pearl's. I'm Pearl. Sit anywhere you like. Are you gentlemen hungry?"

"I'm so hungry I could eat an old leather boot with the foot still in it," Lou says.

"It'd taste better than what you've been feeding us," I say, sitting down and taking off my hat.

Lou hooks a thumb at me as she takes the other seat at the table. "Don't mind him. He fairly lives to complain."

"Don't judge me unless you've had his hog and hominy."

Pearl shakes her head. "I'm afraid I don't have any hog or hominy. But I do have a beef stew and some fresh bread to dunk in it."

My stomach growls again, loudly.

"I'll take that as a yes." She looks at Lou. "And how about you, sir?" She gets kind of a funny look on her face as she says that and takes a second look at Lou.

"No sirs here," Lou says. "I'm Lou and the disreputable-looking one with the long, ratty hair is Ace."

"Ratty?" Pearl says. "As the Lord is my witness, I would give my right arm for hair like that."

I give Lou a smug look.

"Will you gentlemen also be taking rooms?"

"Yes, we will," Lou says.

Pearl brings us food and then pulls up a chair and sits down to talk. "The meals and the beds are on the house," she says. "I saw what you two did, rescuing Annie and her little girl from those ruffians."

"I get the feeling this isn't the first time you've had trouble with them," Lou says.

I look at Lou, more than a little surprised. Sure, Lou talked my ears off when it was just me and her out there, but around others she usually keeps most of her sentences down about the grunt level.

"It's not, and it won't be the last."

"You heard the old sheriff quit?" Lou asks.

"News travels fast in a place this small."

"Then you also heard Annie asked Ace here to be the new sheriff."

"I did." She studies Lou's scowl for a moment, then says, "I get the feeling you'd rather your friend didn't take the job."

"You're damn...I mean, darned right." She turns her scowl on me. "You don't know Ace, so you have no idea how young and eager he is. I wouldn't be surprised if he takes it."

"He seems a very capable young man," Pearl says, looking me up and down. I get the strangest feeling they've forgotten I can hear them, talking about me like I'm not here.

"Oh, he's capable all right, just not that smart about some things. He has a way of getting himself into trouble."

Now I have to say something. "Hold on there, Lou. I'm sitting right here. I can hear you, you know."

"It won't do any good though, will it?" Lou scratches underneath her eye patch and looks back at Pearl.

"I don't want to seem rude, ma'am," she says. "But why don't you and the rest of these folks just take Dace Jackson's money and get the hell out of Dodge? Surely you know how powerful he is, how many hired guns he has."

"None of us here are blind to how dire our situation is," Pearl replies.

"But you're still staying."

"We are," she says proudly, holding her chin up high. "You're new here, so I don't expect you to understand, but there's something different, something special about Lily Creek."

"I'll grant you it's a pretty spot—"

"It's not the beauty that makes it special, but the people. People hold together here, more than anywhere else I've ever been. They look out for each other. They don't...they don't judge you, no matter who you are or where you've come from. A thing like that, it's worth fighting for, don't you think?"

"But is it worth dying for?"

23

After eating, Lou and I walk down the main street and I'm struck by how different this town is from so many I've been in. Most towns are slapped together in a few days, thrown up quick to take advantage of some nearby gold strike or something. Abandoned just as quick too, when the strike peters out.

Lily Creek isn't like that. For one thing the buildings are square. They're solid. Some of them have stone foundations. Nearly everything is painted. There are flowers growing in front of people's houses. There's no garbage anywhere. I don't even see anyone spitting in the street.

On the edge of town is the church. People are streaming through the door. It looks like the whole town is showing up. We head inside and there's probably sixty or seventy people in there, including better than a half dozen kids. They all stop talking and turn and look at us. Annie waves from the front row, her two children sitting beside her, their faces all fresh scrubbed and clean clothes on.

Standing up at the front of the church are three men. One of them is the blacksmith, though he's wearing a white shirt and a black broadcloth coat now, his hair still wet and combed back. He waves us to come on up to the front.

We make it up to the first pew and then Lou sits down. "What're you doing?" I whisper to her. I can feel everybody staring at me.

"It ain't me they asked to be sheriff," she whispers back. "Good luck."

Cursing her under my breath I walk up and join the men. I look them over. The other two look to be farmers, judging by the callouses on their hands and the dirt under their fingernails. None of them look like preachers. At least not like the preachers I'm used to. Maybe the town doesn't have one.

The blacksmith puts his hand on my shoulder and faces the gathered people. "This is Ace," he says. "By now you all know what he did."

The door opens and the banker walks in. He makes his way up the aisle and comes up to stand at the front with the rest of us. He hooks his thumbs in the little pockets on his vest and says, "I apologize for my lateness. Please proceed, Ancil."

The look Ancil gives Herm isn't all that friendly. He continues. "I'm not much for fancy talk, so I'll say it straight out. We got you here to decide for yourself if we should offer the position of sheriff to Ace. Now that Tom has up and quit."

Several people start talking at once, but Herm steps forward and holds up his hands for silence. They taper off.

"Friends and neighbors, good people of Lily Creek. Before we can make a decision of this magnitude, I think it behooves us to learn a little more about Ace, don't you? A few questions, so we may discern his character. Or lack thereof."

Annie glares at him, but he ignores her.

"If no one objects, I shall begin," Herm says. He turns to me. "Do you have any references, young man? Someone who can speak on your behalf?"

I'm not sure what to say, but Lou does.

"I'll speak for him," she says, standing up.

The look Herm gives her, well, it's the same look a man gives a cockroach right before he stomps on it. "And who might you be?"

"I'm Lou. I run cargo with my mule team. Ace rode shotgun for me on the way up here." She looks out over the crowd. "He's a man to ride the river with and that's all I got to say about it." She sits back down.

"Well, that was certainly enlightening," Herm says. His lip curls when he says it.

"It's good enough for me," Annie says.

"Me too," Ancil puts in.

Herm holds up his hands for silence again. I've heard about this thing they do some places, where they tar and feather a man and run him out of town. I wonder why no one's done that to Herm yet. I barely met him and I think he'd look fine in a new tar-and-feather suit.

"While I am sure you are a fine muleteer," he says to Lou, his tone saying he's sure of just about everything but that, "I don't believe that qualifies you to make a judgment on who should be our next sheriff."

Lou crosses her arms and gives him a dark look. I'm glad she's not carrying her whip. Herm might be missing an ear right about now.

"My concern," Herm says, holding up one pudgy hand, "is that we know nothing about this man. He is a complete stranger."

"Everyone's a stranger till you get to know them," Ancil says in his deep voice.

Herm acts like he didn't hear him, but continues on. "Furthermore, unless my eyes deceive me, he is a half-breed. Is this the man we want guarding our children?"

"And you're a purebred idiot," Lou growls. "Unless my eye deceives me. Which it don't."

Herm scowls at her and looks like he wants to respond, but contains himself. "As an outsider, I would be grateful if you kept your comments to yourself, sir. This does not concern you."

"What difference does it make if he's a half-breed?" Annie says. "A man's heritage has no bearing on his character."

Others nod in agreement with her and I can see that Herm made no points with that argument. My opinion of this town goes up a few notches. It's like Pearl said. I see her in the second row and she gives me a look that says I told you so.

Annie's expression gets a little darker and she gestures at her two children. "What's next, Herm? Will you doubt the character of Camila and Diego here because they were born to Mexican parents? Are they to be found lacking as members of this town?"

I'd wondered before about the children, them being so much darker-skinned than Annie. Wondered also if she had a husband somewhere I hadn't met yet. Them being orphans that she took in clears things up a great deal.

Now there's some unhappy muttering from the crowd and Herm can see he has to talk fast to cover up his mistake. "Now I didn't mean that at all, Miss Annie. I only said that…I wanted to make sure because we know nothing of this man."

"That's not true," Annie says stoutly. "We know a lot about him. We know he's the kind of man who stands up for women and children, who puts himself at risk to do the right thing. If you ask me, we don't need to know anything else."

More nodding and talking. Herm's a fool if he can't see he's lost this argument.

Herm apparently isn't that kind of fool because he flutters his hands and lowers his head. "Since it appears I am in the minority here, I rescind my doubts and acquiesce to the will of my friends and neighbors. However, I believe we should make certain Ace is in possession of all the pertinent facts before we ask him if he will take the job."

He looks them over and when no one objects he turns to me. "Do you know who Dace Jackson is?"

"I know of him."

"So you have some idea of the considerable resources he can bring to bear when something stands in the way of what he wants?"

"If that means do I know that he has a whole mess of hired guns at hand, then yes, I do. I was there and saw some for myself."

"And you know that he is a man who is used to getting his way?"

"In my experience, rich men usually are. That doesn't mean we have to roll over for them."

"No, no indeed, it does not. But it does mean that this position comes with a considerable amount of danger, far more than you are probably used to."

"Maybe," I say, thinking about a certain Aztec god and an angry Mexican general.

"And are you also aware that this is a poor town, and this job pays little more than room and board?" He gives me a sly look. "You will be risking your life for a pittance."

Before I can answer, Annie stands up again. "That part isn't true. We can offer you a thousand dollars in gold."

The room goes utterly silent.

24

Herm looks like a steer that got hit with a hammer right between the eyes. He seems to be having trouble getting the words to come out of his mouth.

"Did you say...a *thousand* dollars?" he croaks.

"I did," Annie replies.

Herm takes a hankie from his pocket and wipes his forehead. "That is...that is quite a sum. May I ask how you came to be in possession of so much gold?"

"It was old Joe's."

"Let me clarify this. Old Joe left you a thousand dollars when he died?"

"He did." Annie looks at me. "Joe Winter founded Lily Creek. He didn't have any family and he loved this place more than anything. I took care of him at the end, when he was dying, and right before he went he told me about the gold." She turns and looks out over the crowd.

"He said I should keep the gold quiet, and use it if there was ever an emergency. Well, I think this counts as an emergency."

"If this is true," Herm says, causing Annie to turn and glare at him again, "then why is the gold not in the safe at my bank, where it would be safe?"

"It's safe where it is, well-hidden."

"Are you sure it is a thousand-dollars' worth? It is possible you are mistaken about its value."

"I know what gold's worth all right," she says. "And old Joe said that's how much it was. That's good enough for me." She turns those green eyes on me. "Is that good enough for you, or do I have to get it out and show you?"

"I believe you," I say. I notice Lou shaking her head, but I ignore her. Annie's got an honest face. I trust her.

Annie pulls the star out of her pocket. "Will you take the job, then?"

Every eye swings to me. Suddenly I don't feel so sure.

"Oh, now, what's wrong with you people?" Herm blurts out. "You're looking at this no-account drifter like he's our lord and savior, like one man can stand up to a hundred. Why don't we talk about what he and his one-eyed friend really did today? What they did is go and stir up a hornets' nest of trouble. They went and angered Dace. Now there'll be hell to pay. He might take his offer back altogether and leave us all with nothing."

Annie shakes her finger at him. "If you want to take Dace's money and run off, you go right ahead, Herm. But I for one am not about to run. Lily Creek is my home." She gestures at the kids. "It's *our* home. And we're not letting that scoundrel run us off!"

Scattered clapping and a few cheers greet her words. Herm gives her a black look. "You won't do those orphans any good if you're dead, Annie."

That shuts everyone up. They get real somber. "Don't talk like that," the blacksmith says. "Not in front of the children, Herm."

"Why not? It's the truth, that's all it is." Herm glowers at all of them. "You think I like it any better than you do? I've built a thriving bank here. I don't want to give it up and run. But what choice do I have? What choice do any of us have? You all know Dace. You know what he's capable of. His men will kill us all and that will be that. I say we take his money and be glad we're getting anything."

"Well, I say we fight," Annie says. "These are our homes. This is our town."

"Fight? Are you touched in the head, woman? Look around you. What do you see here? Do they look like fighters to you?"

I have to agree with him there. I see farmers, shop keepers. Simple folk. Not that many of fighting age even.

"I'm not giving up," Annie says stubbornly, crossing her arms. "I'll fight if necessary."

Behind her, the little old white-haired lady I saw earlier shakes her cane in the air. "I'll fight too!" she yells.

"You'll help, won't you, Ace?" Annie asks. "You'll take the job?"

With those big eyes on me my knees get a little weak. It's hard to think straight. I open my mouth, but before I can say anything, Lou gets up and grabs my arm.

"Let me talk to you for a minute." She pulls me aside and in a low voice asks, "You're not that big a fool, are you?"

"But they need help. There's orphans and little old ladies and everything."

"You're pretty flashy with those guns, I can see that. But you can't take on an army."

"Not alone. But maybe with your help."

"I may be crazy, but not crazy enough to get myself killed in a hopeless cause."

"I'm going to do it."

"Answer me this, Ace. Are you doing it for the town? Or for her?"

"For the town."

"Sure."

"Okay, maybe for her."

"How did that end last time?"

Yeah, I told Lou about Victoria. "That hurts, you know." Lou just stares at me. "This isn't the same thing at all."

"You sure about that?"

"Yeah, I'm sure. Orphans? Little old ladies?"

"You're hopeless, you know that?"

"Does that mean you'll stay and help?"

"It doesn't mean anything," she grumbles. "Go on and take the job then. I've said my piece."

We turn back to the others. "I'll do it," I say.

Annie flashes me one of her brilliant smiles and comes up and pins the sheriff's badge on my shirt. It feels strange, that's for sure. Being called sheriff isn't something I ever thought I'd experience.

The meeting starts to break up then, people filing out of the church. When I step outside Herm collars me. "I don't believe she has the money at all. You should get out while you can. Get on your horse and ride away."

"Mister, I sure don't like you."

He frowns at me. "What's that got to do with anything?"

"I don't know, but there it is."

"If you do this, you'll die."

I poke him in the chest with my finger. I'm the sheriff now. I can get away with it. "You're awful keen to see everyone leave. What's your angle in this?"

"I don't have an angle. I don't want to see people die, that's all."

"Maybe."

"You're as dumb as the rest of them."

"Probably."

"Don't say I didn't warn you." He turns and stalks off.

25

When I come in for breakfast the next morning I find Lou already up. Pearl is sitting with her and the two are drinking coffee and laughing. They look up, see me, and laugh even harder.

"What's so funny?" I grumble, sitting down and reaching for a coffee cup.

"Nothing," they say together and laugh some more.

At most I get a mouthful of coffee out of the pot. "Nice of you to leave me some."

"Cheer up," Pearl says, standing up. "I'll make you some more." She takes the pot and heads for the kitchen.

"How long till you leave town?" I ask Lou.

"I like this place. I may stick around for another day." Lou grins at me. "I didn't know you were that anxious to get rid of me."

I don't reply, just give her a look to let her know I'm not amused.

"Who crapped in your flapjacks this morning?"

"Maybe it's being laughed at first thing, before I even get a cup of coffee."

"Don't bullshit me, Ace. I know you too well. Something's eating you."

I look around to make sure Pearl can't hear us. "I'm worried."

"I'm not surprised."

"How am I supposed to protect a whole town by myself?"

The look on Lou's face says she's dying to say 'I told you so.' But she's smart enough not to. Instead she says, "Don't."

"What?"

"Leave. Saddle up that ugly nag you call a horse and ride away. There's no one stopping you."

I scowl at her. "I can't do that."

"Someone pointing a gun at you?"

"No."

"Then you can."

"I said I'd help. If I leave now, I'll never be able to live with myself."

"If you stay, living with yourself might not be a problem for all that long."

"Don't you have anything useful to say?"

"Not really." Lou leans back in her chair and hooks her thumbs in her belt. There's times I swear I forget she's a woman, she looks and acts so much like a man. "I'm just pointing out to you that you have choices, even if you act like you don't."

She reaches into her pocket for her tobacco but while she's getting it out she looks around and sees that there's no spittoon. With a sigh, she puts the tobacco away.

"You didn't talk them into staying. They made that choice themselves. Seems to me they had it made before you ever showed up," she says.

"I don't really see where you're going with this."

"Just this. They made their choice. You made your choice. Do what you can and stop worrying about how it turns out."

I rub my face. "Thanks, I guess."

"You're welcome," she says with a smile. "All my advice comes with a money-back guarantee."

Pearl comes out of the kitchen then, carrying the coffeepot and a platter piled with eggs, ham, and flapjacks. The food and the coffee help, I have to admit. I feel a whole lot better afterwards. I thank Pearl for the food and put my hat on.

"I think I'll take a look around," I say.

Neither one of them is listening to me. They're talking about Pearl's dress.

"I just got the fabric in two weeks ago," Pearl says. "I only finished the dress two days ago."

I go back to my room and fetch my rifles, then I walk down the street. Everyone I pass is all kinds of friendly, the men wanting to shake my hand, the women smiling. It doesn't help my mood. They're counting on me to save their town and all I can think is I wish I'd never come to Lily Creek. Then I wouldn't know anything about this.

The bank is right before the sheriff's office and Herm is unlocking the door when I walk by. He gives me a sour look when he sees me and that cheers me up some. I don't like the man and I don't trust him. If I can foul whatever plans he's got going, that'll mean something.

"Good morning, Herm!" I call out. "How are you today?"

He grumbles something I can't quite hear. I follow him into the bank, look around and whistle.

"This is quite a bank you got here, Herm. Quite a bank."

It's actually just one room with a desk and a safe against the back wall.

"What do you want, Sheriff?" he says, sitting down at his desk. I take the chair in front of it and put my feet up on his desk.

"I just wanted to stop in and assure you that I'm on the job and you don't have to worry yourself a bit about the safety of your bank. I'm right next door and I'll keep my eyes on you the whole time."

Herm doesn't look too happy about that. He doesn't look too happy about my boots on his desk, either. Some people always have to see the dark side of things.

"That's quite all right, Sheriff. I'm sure you have bigger problems to deal with."

"Aw shucks, I'll never be too busy to stop in and check up on you, Herm. You know that."

He gives me what's supposed to be a smile, but is really just bared teeth. "If you're quite done, I have a great deal of work to do."

"Oh, am I keeping you from your work?" I say innocently. "I wouldn't want that. I know what an important person you are."

I get up and go to the door where I turn back and touch the brim of my hat. "It's been a pleasure, Herm."

26

There isn't much to the sheriff's office. A cell just about big enough for a man to lie down in, if he's kind of short. It's covered in thick dust, so it clearly doesn't get much use. There's also a desk, two chairs, a lantern and a pot-bellied stove with a coffee pot on it, a tin cup sitting beside it. There's some pegs set in the wall and I hang the Winchester and the Spencer rifles on them.

I pick up the coffee pot and pour some foul-looking sludge into the cup. It's purely awful and I can barely choke it down. Maybe I shouldn't drink it. Who knows how old it is?

I pour the rest into my cup and drink it fast. It doesn't hurt as much that way.

Why'd I drink that? I wonder. Maybe Lou's right. Maybe there's something wrong with me.

I go to the back door and step out. Lily Creek is a one-street town. There aren't any buildings behind the sheriff's office, just some grass, aspen saplings and a few fir trees. About fifty yards away is the creek itself.

I walk on down to the creek. It's a pretty spot for a town, that's for sure. Nice little valley with good water. High enough up that the summers are cool and the grass is thick. Not so high that it's snowed in all winter. Aspen groves. Pine trees. Granite outcroppings in the distance. A few of the aspen leaves are starting to turn yellow.

Down a ways, on the other side of the creek, I see a man slinking around in the shadows.

He's surely up to no good.

I cross the creek and sneak up on him. Whoever he is, he's dressed all in buckskins and wearing a coonskin hat. And he's carrying a rifle. He's sneaking from one tree to the next, the rifle ready in both hands.

He peers around a tree and raises the rifle to his shoulder.

I cross the distance between us in a few quick strides and put a pistol up to his head, right behind his ear, where I'm sure he can hear me cock it.

"Lower your gun, stranger. Nice and easy so I don't accidentally shoot you."

"Dadgummit!" He lowers his rifle and spins on me. "You gone and skeered him off! What am I gonna eat tonight now?"

He looks to be about eighty, his skin browned to the color of old leather by the sun. His rifle looks like it might be older than he is.

"Scared who off? Who were you aiming to shoot, old timer?"

"Not who, you idjit! What!"

"What?"

"A squirrel. And not just any squirrel, mind you, but the smartest squirrel there ever was. I bin hunting that squirrel for two years and I finally had him. Dead to rights! Until you snuck up and ruint ever'thing."

"You were hunting a squirrel?" I feel a little dumb. I should have realized that.

"I was gonna eat him. I was gonna boil him down to mush and have him fer my dinner." The old man is sporting a single tooth, right in the center on the top. That explains the whole boiling to mush thing.

"I thought you were fixing to shoot someone. Thought maybe you were one of Dace Jackson's men."

His whole faces wrinkles up in a frown. "Do I *look* like one of them snakes?" he cries.

"Not much."

"You're none too bright, are you?"

"I'm the new sheriff."

"I heard about you. I been expecting you, actually."

"Why would you be expecting me?"

He plants his rifle butt in the ground and draws his bony old shoulders back, straightening up as best he can and giving me a salute. "Virgil Weathercock, that's my name. I heered yore looking for men."

"For what?"

"To fight."

"Uh...no offense, but aren't you a little old?"

"No offense, Sheriff, but ain't you a little young?" he snaps. His eyes are very bright underneath bushy white eyebrows.

"I'm a full grown man."

"And so am I! Listen, you little whippersnapper, I was shootin' and fightin' before your daddy was a gleam in your grandpappy's eyes."

That's what I'm worried about. But its' not all I'm worried about.

I eye his rifle. It looks like it's held together with some bits of wire and a whole lot of hope. "What about that rifle? You have anything else to shoot with?"

"You think ol' Hilda here can't shoot straight, is that it?"

"*Does* it still shoot?"

"Why don't you go fetch a rifle and we'll see how well Hilda shoots, you young rascal."

"Now that's not hardly fair," I protest.

"Giving up already, is you?"

"That's not it at all. I just…"

"Just what? Afraid to get your ass handed to you by an old codger?"

I've had about enough of this. Time to shut this old fool up. I'm not taking it easy on him.

When I get to the sheriff's office I find Lou in there. She's built a fire in the potbellied stove and is making a fresh batch of coffee.

"What are you doing here?" I ask her.

She looks at the coffeepot in her hand, then at me, her expression wondering if I'm simple or just stupid. "What are *you* doing here? I thought you were going to ride out."

"You wouldn't believe me if I told you," I say, taking the Spencer down from the pegs on the wall. "Make some for me. I'll be right back."

When I get back to Virgil he says, "Pick your target."

About sixty yards off there's a whitish rock on the ground. "How about that rock?"

"That's it?" he says scornfully. "You ain't even going to make it challenging?"

Instead of answering, I shoot. The rock flies up into the air.

Virgil raises up his long gun, sights for a moment, then fires. The rock cracks in half, the pieces flying.

"Okay, old timer. I take it back. You can shoot."

"Not so fast, sonny. I ain't done teaching you manners yet."

"Why don't you pick the next target then?"

He gets a big, loopy grin on his face, his loose lips peeling back to show a frightening quantity of yellowed gums. "Now you're talking."

He digs a pair of spectacles out of his pocket and wraps the loops over his ears. He peers off into the distance, then points. "That squirrel."

I can't see it at first. "There's no squirrel there."

"Hell there ain't. You're just afraid you can't hit it."

I squint. Sure enough, there's a squirrel on a tree branch about a hundred yards out, chewing on a pine cone. "There's no way you can hit that, Virgil."

"You mean no way *you* can hit that. I kin shoot him in the eye."

"Go ahead, then."

He shakes his head. "Nope. You go first." He hefts his rifle. "When you miss, then I'll pop 'im."

It's a long shot and a small target. I raise up the Spencer, noticing that Virgil sights in at the same time. His tongue's sticking out between his teeth and he makes this little whistling sound as he breathes.

I fire. The squirrel drops the pine cone and takes off along the branch. It gets about three steps and Virgil fires. The squirrel falls to the ground.

I can't believe my eyes.

"Close your mouth, sonny. You're drawing flies."

I look at Virgil. "That was some shooting."

"You're damn right it was." He pats me on the arm. "Don't take it too hard, sonny. You never really had a chance."

"My name's Ace."

"And it's a fine name, sonny."

"But you're probably not going to use it, are you?"

"Probably not, sonny."

"If you've got something to ride, I'll take you up on that help. Be ready in ten minutes." I head back to the sheriff's office.

27

Lou has the coffeepot on and is sitting behind the desk, her feet up on it.

I tap the star on my chest. "You're sitting in my chair."

She points at the other chair. "How do you know that's not your chair?"

The seat is split on the other chair and it looks like a couple of the legs are about to fall off. "I'm the sheriff. The good chair is my chair."

"Fair enough."

She makes no sign of moving. I put the Spencer up on the wall and go ahead and sit down in the other chair. One of the legs is too short and I come pretty close to spilling on the floor. Lou chuckles.

"I heard shooting out there. Did you already get yourself in trouble?" she asks.

"It was some old coot named Virgil."

"Pearl told me about him. Hails from Tennessee. Claims he fought in the War of 1812."

"I can believe it."

"She said he's got a little log cabin up the mountainside. Makes his own corn liquor and keeps the squirrel population down."

"He wants to help fight Jackson."

"See? You got your first recruit."

"Dace doesn't know what he's up against."

"Now you've gone and pissed him off, what do you think he'll try next? I'm talking about Jackson, not Virgil."

"I don't know. Probably send some more men over. They'll be expecting trouble. Won't be able to catch them off guard this time."

"What are you going to do?"

"Catch them off guard." I stand up and take the Winchester off the wall. It shoots faster than the Spencer, better for close up work against more targets. "Save me some of that coffee."

I fetch Coyote from the corral. Someone's been brushing him and gave him a pot of oats. He's not too happy about being disturbed, but he only tries to bite me once, so it's a good day all and all.

I ride out of town, following the road that heads west, toward the Hashknife outfit. Virgil's waiting and falls in behind me.

There's a little pass they have to go through to get to Lily Creek. I point out to Virgil where I want him, then leave Coyote in the trees and make my way into some jumbled rocks on one side of the pass. Then I settle down to wait.

A couple hours go by and here comes a half dozen riders. I see who's in the lead and start to smile. It's my lucky day.

The one in the lead is Wilkins.

When they get close I stand up, the Winchester across my chest.

"That's close enough, boys."

They rein in their horses and look up, startled.

"You should pay more attention, you know. You could ride right into an ambush," I say.

Hands start to reach for weapons. I point the rifle at them. "The first one touches iron gets a piece of lead as a going-away present."

"There's six of us an' only one of him," one of them says. He's smoking a thin cigar.

I shift the Winchester and fire once. The cigar explodes in a cloud of tobacco. "No smoking in Lily Creek."

Everyone freezes.

"This here is private property and you boys are trespassing. What you want to do is turn around and head on back home. Tell your boss you got lost. Tell him you were too tired to roust women and children today."

Wilkins has been squinting at me and now he says, "Don't I know you?"

I shift the barrel over to point at him and show him all my teeth. "It's about time, Wilkins, old friend. I was starting to get hurt feelings, thinking you didn't care enough to remember me."

"I *do* know you. You're that half-breed from that ranch in Texas."

"That's me, all right. The half-breed from Texas. And you're the lily-livered wood rat from that same ranch. It's a mighty small world, isn't it?"

He gives me a yellow smile. "You better hightail it out of here. Last I heard you're a wanted man, a cattle rustler. Could be someone will try to collect the reward."

I pull back my duster and show him the star pinned on my shirt. "What's this?" I say like I just discovered it there. "Why, it's a sheriff's star. It says you're the rustler. Maybe you're about to get your own wanted poster. Or maybe you're about to get shot while trying to escape."

His eyes bug out. It's not a pleasant sight. "They made you sheriff? But you're just a no-account half-breed." He sounds so bothered by this I almost feel sorry for him. He looks like he's really having trouble fitting this into his tiny, wrinkled brain.

"It's a funny world, isn't it? One day you're fixing to get a man hung for no reason and the next he's pointing a rifle at you. There's no figuring it out." I snap my fingers. "Just figured it out. I know what it is. It's not me who's no-account, it's you. Take some friendly advice, Wilkins. Pull your poke and drag your freight. Get out while you still can. I've got a powerful urge to shoot you and I don't know how long I can hold out."

"You shoot me here in front of these witnesses and it's murder. Ain't no other word for it!"

"But I got my own witness," I reply. "Virgil!"

Virgil stands up from his hiding spot in the rocks on the other side of the pass and waves his coonskin cap. He makes a rude sound with his lips and takes bead on the men.

"That's enough, Virgil!" I call. "Don't go shooting them before they get a chance to run away!"

"But I want to shoot me a skunk!" he protests.

"You'll get your chance, I reckon. Some of these men look like the slow-learning type."

"Promise me I get to shoot the one with the yeller hair?"

"Why that one, Virgil?"

"Somethin' in his face I don't like. I had a mule with a face like that. I always hated that critter."

The yellow-haired man is looking strangely uncomfortable about our conversation.

"Okay, if he causes any problem I'll leave him for you to shoot. I promise. Now back down."

Virgil lowers his rifle. "Cain't say I saw the world coming to this, when some uppity Injun barely off his mama's teat is telling me who I can and can't shoot." But he sinks back down out of sight behind the rocks.

The yellow-haired man looks relieved but he keeps throwing glances at the last spot he saw Virgil.

"Reckon you all will be moseying along now," I say.

"I seen enough for one day," the yellow-haired man says, turning his horse. "I'm heading back to the ranch." All the others except for Wilkins start to follow him.

"Where you going?" Wilkins hollers. "You listen to me, if you ride away now you're out of a job. Every one of you. You'll draw no pay neither."

"Pay don't spend when you're dead," the yellow-haired man yells back.

Wilkins swears at them a couple times, then turns and looks at me. "This ain't over."

"Really, Wilkins, I knew you'd say that. Why, it's the same thing yesterday's scoundrel said. You two ought to get together and work up some new patter. It's downright tiresome listening to you repeat each other."

Now he's swearing at me, something about what I ought to do with my own mother. It's shocking, really. I lift the barrel a couple inches and shoot his hat off.

"No one should speak like that about anyone's mama," I say. "And you don't even know mine."

He swears some more, his face turning an awful shade of red. When he leans down out of the saddle to pick up his hat I shoot it again so it flies a couple feet further on.

"Nope," I say. "You've been a bad boy, talking about my mama that way. You ride on home without a hat and think real hard on the error of your ways."

He spurs his horse savagely and rides away. Virgil comes out of hiding and walks over to me.

"We shoulda just shot them all," he says. "Make things easier later on."

"You might have a problem, you know that, Virgil?"

"None I can't handle with my squirrel gun." He lifts the coonskin hat and scratches his head. When he does a powerful stink flows out.

"That smells purely terrible," I tell him, taking a step back. "You sure that's made out of just the skin, or you wearing the whole carcass on your head?"

He sniffs it. "It's a bit ripe, I allow. Maybe even what you'd call fragrant." He sniffs again. "But I like it. It's earthy."

"Rotten is the word you're looking for, Virgil."

"Uppity young pup," he grumbles, settling it back on his head.

28

Figuring they won't try anything else for the rest of the day, I ride back into town, Virgil following on his mule.

"A mule is the worst sort of animal ever created," I tell him. "You should meet my friend Lou. He's partial to mules too."

"Lou sounds like a right sort of feller."

Virgil peels off before we hit town. "Since you run off my dinner, I still got to find something to eat."

"Why don't you eat that mule?"

"You ever et mule?" he asks. "You won't twice. Besides, I need Elmo here to draw my plow so I can plant my corn. How else am I to make corn likker without corn?"

"I never thought of it that way. I appreciate your help back there."

"I'd appreciate if next time you'd let me shoot a couple of them," he calls over his shoulder.

Now Lou's sitting out on the porch in front of the sheriff's office. In my chair. The one with four good legs. She's tilted back against the wall and has her hat down over her face. Leaning against the wall next to her is her double-barreled shotgun, Betsy.

I climb down off Coyote and get up on the porch. "That's the sheriff's chair. Only the sheriff gets to sit there."

She lifts her hat and spits a brown glob at me. Or almost at me. It just misses me and splats on the porch. "Oops," she says. "Thought you was the spittoon."

"Tobacco's a foul habit."

"Yep."

"And we don't have a spittoon."

"Yep."

"Don't you have something better to do?"

She scratches under one arm and makes a satisfied noise when she's done. "It's my day of rest."

"You're leaving tomorrow, right?"

"I saw one of the shoes on Old Nibs was loose. Told the smith to pull all of them and replace them." She smiles, showing me brown teeth. "Told him to put it on your bill."

"I'm not paying to shoe your mule. I hate that mule. That critter's evil."

"You're still sore that he kicked you? That's just a sign of his affection is all."

"That doesn't change anything."

"You owe me. Consider this partial payment."

"I don't owe you."

"You will. Same thing."

"What's that mean?"

She stands and stretches. "I've decided to stick around for a couple of days. I can see you're the type of man with a tendency to fall down the well trying to get the chicken out. Could be you'll need my help getting out of the muck."

That makes me feel better, I have to admit. At least to myself. I'm not saying it out loud. Lou will only get all puffed up. Virgil's help is better than nothing, but I'm thinking he's not right in the head.

"You're going over to see Miss Annie now," Lou says.

It's not a question. "What makes you so sure of that?"

"Oh, come on, Ace," she says, patting my cheek. "I thought we were done with secrets between us. Any fool with eyes can see you're sweet on her."

"She's a nice enough lady…"

Lou guffaws. She's really good at it. I already feel a little stupid for what I said.

"I was going to go over there, but now I think I'll go into the office. *My* office." I snatch up the chair Lou was sitting in. "With *my* chair. I believe there's some paperwork I need to do." I pull open the door and go in. Lou follows me.

"Don't be any more of an idiot than you already are. If you like the girl, go tell her. You never know when you'll get another chance."

"Don't bother me," I say gruffly. "I have work to do." There's a small stack of wanted posters on the desk and I sit down and start going through them. A man in my position ought to familiarize himself with the local bandits, I figure.

Lou pulls up the other chair and plops down. For some reason it doesn't almost drop her on the floor. "Lookit you, playing sheriff. It's mighty impressive, I'll grant you that."

"You oughtn't be interfering with a peace officer performing his duties," I tell her without looking up from the wanted posters. Geez, these things are really awful. Most look like they were drawn by an addled child. I wouldn't recognize the men drawn on them if they walked up and shot me in the foot.

"Didn't you just do those duties? Didn't I hear shots way off in the distance?"

I look at her finally. "There's more to being sheriff than shooting."

"Is there? And what would that be?"

"This," I say, holding up the posters.

"And?"

"And other stuff. Like making sure no drifters are causing trouble in the saloon."

"Lily Creek has no saloon."

Shoot. I forgot that. "There's other places drifters could be causing troubles." I open the desk drawer. There's a dried-out lizard in there, a pretty big one. I pull it out and look at it. Two of its legs are painted red. Why would anyone do that? What was the old sheriff up to in here?

"Just go talk to her."

"You're not going to leave me alone, are you?"

She hooks her thumbs in her suspenders. "I got nothing else to do."

"Fine. Have it your way." I put the lizard back in the drawer and close it. I get up and go to the door. "Don't touch anything in my office while I'm gone."

29

I walk on down to Annie's house. She's out working in her garden, tying up tomato plants.

"Is this one of them tomato worms?" Camila calls out to her. The little girl is leaning in close to one of the tomato plants, looking at something.

Annie looks over. "It is. Pluck it off and give it to the chickens."

"I don't wanna touch it. It's gross!"

"It won't hurt you, child. It's just a caterpillar. But if you leave it there it'll eat up our tomato plants and then you won't get any tomatoes."

Squinching up her face, the little girl takes hold of the thing and pulls it off the plant, then runs off toward where some chickens are scratching in the dirt. Her little brother takes off after her, yelling, "I wanna see! I wanna see the chickens eat it!"

Annie brushes the dirt off her hands and turns to me. She's wearing a big, floppy hat that you could shade two people under, and her sleeves are pushed up to show her forearms. "What have you been up to today, Ace?"

"Not much. I went for a ride."

"I heard shots." A little line appears between her eyebrows and she looks me over. "I was worried about you. I'm glad to see you're okay."

"Oh, that," I say casually. "Just running off some varmints."

"The two-legged kind?"

"Maybe."

"Any problems?"

"At first. But I helped them see reason and everything turned out fine."

She gets a troubled look on her face. "I know you act like it's nothing, but I worry about you. I fear we pushed you into something that could get you hurt."

"Not true. I'm doing it for the money."

She gives me a look. "That's not true and we both know it." She puts her hand on my arm. It feels warm and comforting. "You act tough, but I can see through it. I can see what kind of man you are, Ace. I know what a good heart you have."

Having her this close to me makes it hard to think. I want to bolt like a frightened filly, but I remind myself that I'm Ace Lone Wolf. Not afraid of anything.

"No offense, Miss Annie, but you might be mistaken. I'm just a drifter who's handy with a gun."

"I thought we were past that Miss Annie nonsense. It's just Annie. And I don't believe I am mistaken. I'm an excellent judge of character and I can tell that is something you have a great deal of."

"Well, I won't argue with you, especially seeing's how you're my boss and all."

"And don't you forget it." She smiles at me. It's an amazing smile, like the sun coming out after a long, cloudy day. I guess I could stand here for hours looking at that smile.

She waves her hand in front of my face. "Ace? Are you still there?"

I snap out of it. How long was I staring? I think of Lou laughing at me and I look around guiltily to see if anyone saw. "I was thinking about something."

The look in Annie's eyes tells me she's not buying the heifer I'm selling.

"You have beautiful hair," she says out of nowhere, startling me so I jump just a little.

"You think so?" Except for Pearl yesterday I don't believe anyone has ever said anything about my hair other than it makes me look like a wild savage and I ought to cut it if I want to pass for a civilized man.

"I do." She reaches out partway, then hesitates. "May I?"

I open my mouth and what pops out sounds something like "Blug?"

She laughs. "What was that?"

I clear my throat. My heart is running too fast. "I mean, okay. Whatever." Am I dreaming? Of course you may touch my hair, I think. You may do anything you like. You may take my gun and shoot me through the heart and I can't stop you.

She strokes my hair. "What I would give for hair like this. It's so straight, so soft."

"Your hair's nice too," I blurt out, and immediately regret it. I sound like an idiot. I should stick to 'blug.'

"Oh, that's nice of you to say, but you don't have to. I know it's all ratty and I must look a frightful mess."

"That's not true."

The words come out without my say-so, but they seem to be the right ones because she smiles real big and a little blush gets into her cheeks. "What a sweet thing to say, Ace."

She's close enough that I can see the flecks of blue mixed into her green eyes and I'm wondering if it would be a good idea to say something about it when something runs into my legs from the side, practically knocking me down.

I look down and see that Camila has launched herself at me and has both arms wrapped tight around my leg, grinning up at me. "Ace!" she shouts. "You came to visit!"

Diego comes racing up then. The two of them start pulling on me.

"You have to come see!" Diego shouts. "We found a June bug! We're going to tie a string to him and make him fly around!"

"You better go with them," Annie says, laughing. "They'll give you no peace, otherwise."

As they're dragging me away she calls out to me. "Plan to come for dinner tomorrow night."

30

When I walk into the boarding house near sundown Lou and Pearl are sitting together at a table, their heads together, thick as thieves. They look up, see me, and start laughing.

"Again?" I say. "A man could get ideas in his head from you laughing at him all the time."

"Who says we're laughing at you?"

"Who says you aren't?"

"Don't give us so much to laugh about," Lou says.

"Shouldn't be laughing at the sheriff. It undermines my authority."

"We wouldn't want that, Sheriff sir," Lou says with her most serious face.

The whole time Pearl is fighting a serious case of the giggles and she's not winning.

"Oh, just go on and let it out," I grumble. "You might as well laugh to my face."

"He's just like you said, Lou," she says, wiping her eyes. She looks back up at me. "She does the best imitation of you."

I pull out a chair and plunk down. "Don't I get some board with my room?"

That brings a fresh wave of laughing, but Pearl gets up and heads for the kitchen.

"You're a lot grumpier since you become sheriff," Lou says.

"The badge wears heavy."

"How'd your meeting with Annie go?"

"She invited me to dinner tomorrow night."

"So that's what's got you so touchy."

"I'm not touchy."

"As a bear with a sore tooth. There's nothing to be afraid of, you know. She seems like a nice sort. You're not too bad in your own way."

"Is that the best you can come up with? That I'm not too bad?"

"She doesn't know you like I do," Lou says with a wicked smile.

"You're just making my head hurt now," I complain.

Pearl comes back in, toting a platter heavy with grub. "Did I hear tell you're going on a date tomorrow night with Annie?"

"It's not a date. It's just dinner."

"You can call a duck a chicken, but that don't make it a chicken."

"Fine. It's a date. I suppose you're going to tell the whole town."

"I reckon the whole town already knows, Ace. News travels fast around here."

"He's a little nervous," Lou says. "But he doesn't want to let on, so act like you don't notice."

That brings a fresh round of laughter. What made these two decide to gang up on me? I wonder.

"Can we talk about something else?" I say.

"What do you want to talk about?"

That stumps me. I can't think of anything. Not with both of them looking at me anyway, big old grins on their faces.

"I think I'll eat over here." I pick up my plate and go to one of the other tables. They laugh of course. I wonder if I can stay in the livery from here on out. Or maybe Virgil has room in his log cabin.

After I'm done eating, I get up from the table, thank Pearl for the food, and put on my hat.

"Headed out?" Lou asks. She's not smiling now.

I nod.

"You want some help? I can move quiet when I need to."

"I believe you can. And I believe I'll take you up on that offer. But not tonight. It's too soon. They're still licking their wounds and making plans. It's tomorrow night that they'll hit."

"But you're going out tonight anyway."

"There's always the chance I'm wrong."

Coyote isn't all that happy to see me. In fact, he's downright irritable. "I am the law," I tell him. "And the law never sleeps."

Which isn't true. I've seen the law sleep lots of times. But maybe it will ease him a bit.

116

It doesn't. He tries to bite me once and step on me twice. I'm slowed from dinner, but not that slowed and they all miss. I whack him on the neck. "Guess who's not getting the apple I stuck in my pocket?"

Which isn't true, either. I give him the apple anyway. It makes up for some of it, but not all.

The town is quiet, most of the houses dark. As I get off the main street, though, I see a faint light coming through a back window in Herm's place. I don't think much of it and I'm fixing to ride on by when his back door opens and he steps out.

31

I rein in Coyote and sit there in the darkness. Is it a trip to the privy, or something more? I have a feeling he's up to no good. There's something about this man that sticks in my craw.

He soft foots it down to the livery stable, gets his horse out of the corral and saddles it. All of it he does without a light, which makes me even more suspicious. You're up to something, Herm, I think. Something you don't want anyone to know about.

And I aim to find out.

He heads out of town and goes west, with me trailing him about fifty yards back. Once we're away from town he stops and lights this little miner's lantern. I almost laugh out loud. Old Herm's not the sharpest arrow in the quiver.

See, he thinks the lantern means he can see now. But really all it does is make him blind. Sure, he can see in a little ten-foot area, but nothing at all past that. He's killed his night vision. On top of that, he just made himself a target. Light in the darkness is a magnet for bad intentions. Safety lies in darkness. It wraps around you, hides you and makes you safe.

Herm rides west for about fifteen minutes, following a game trail through the pines and up into this little saddle. Someone is waiting there for him. It's Wilkins.

"Put out that damn lantern!" Wilkins barks. "You want to let the whole state know what we're doing here?"

"But it's dark and there's no moon."

"Damned right it's dark. That's why they call it nighttime. How do you know that damned half-breed didn't follow you?"

Damn this and damn that. Sounds to me like old Wilkins needs to learn some new swear words.

"He didn't follow me. I waited until everything was quiet. I was careful." Herm is still holding up the lantern. The light shows the sweat on his face. He's really not cut out for skulking around.

Wilkins draws his gun. "Put out that lantern before I put it out for you."

Reluctantly, Herm douses the lantern. "I don't see what good that does," he grouses. "Now I can't see you."

"You don't need to see me and I sure as hell don't want to see you. Now, give me an update. What's the mood in town?"

"Only one family has left. The rest are staying. It's the new sheriff. They believe he can protect them."

Wilkins swears. "That just shows how stupid they are. He's only one man. We got an army. What can he do?"

Then Herm surprises me, showing a lot more backbone than I gave him credit for. "He's run you boys off twice already."

"He caught us by surprise, damn you. It won't happen again."

"What're you going to do next?"

"We're going to burn them out. But that don't concern you. You just keep doing what we're paying you to do. What are we paying you for anyway? You're about as useless as tits on a bull."

"I'm doing the best I can."

"Well do better! Ain't you a respected banker and all? Don't they listen to you?"

"They did until Ace showed up. Now they listen to him. He and Annie. She's the one whose idea it was to hire him."

"How'd she do that? You said none of them folks have two nickels to rub together."

"She says old man Winter left some gold behind when he died. For an emergency. That's what she's going to pay Ace with."

"She has gold? How much?"

I can hear the change in Wilkins' voice. Funny how quickly gold changes men. Right now I'd bet my last plugged nickel he's wondering if there's some way he can get his hands on it.

"At least a thousand dollars."

"You got any idea where it's hid?"

"I don't know. Must be in her house though. Where else would it be? It's not in the bank, that's for sure."

"Did you see it?"

"She says it's too well hidden to get out easily."

"Now just hold on. You mean that half-breed took a job that's gonna get him killed without ever seeing the money?"

"He did."

"How could anyone be that stupid?"

"I think he's sweet on Annie. That's what I think."

I'm not liking how this conversation is going. It's giving me all kinds of doubts. Annie didn't lie to me about the gold, did she? I mean, I'm not really doing it just for the gold, but the gold sure helps.

Mostly I don't like the idea that I'm being lied to. Again.

"You think she has the gold?"

"I don't know," Herm says. "At first I was sure she was lying, but then I got to thinking. Old man Winter was pretty reclusive. No one knew much about him, but there's talk he came from New York, that his family made some real money in railroads but he had a falling out with his father and left. I suppose he could have brought some of that money with him. And Annie nursed him the whole time he was dying. He might have left it to her."

"Well," Wilkins says, "this changes things. Could be I'll have to pay little Annie a visit."

Wilkins almost gets shot right then and there. Of course, then I'd have to shoot Herm too and that's getting a little too close to outright murder for me. Shooting a man in a fight is one thing. Killing him in the darkness goes against the grain.

They end their meeting a couple minutes later and I cut out and head back to town, too many thoughts weighing down my mind.

32

The next morning I'm finishing up breakfast when Lou comes in. She doesn't look too good, her eyes all bloodshot, her skin kind of gray.

"What happened to you?"

She sits down and reaches for a coffee cup. "I paid a visit to Virgil's cabin."

"You were drinking his moonshine."

She picks up the coffeepot and pours herself a cup. "I don't know. It mighta been kerosene. Tasted like it."

"You should go easy on that stuff. You can see what it's done to Virgil."

"He ain't so bad once you get to know him. His cabin smells like a bear died in there."

"I don't think Virgil believes much in bathing."

"He believes in moonshine."

"And you?"

"Not so much. Not anymore."

"I followed Herm last night. It seems he had a meeting." I tell her what I saw. "What do you think I should do? Should I call him out, expose him in front of the others?"

Lou sets her cup down and rubs her temples. "You do that and he'll just deny it and go underground. You'll learn more if he doesn't know that you know."

"Maybe. I already learned what they're going to try next. I reckon they'll go for the church."

Lou grunts and drinks some more coffee. I get up and put my hat on.

"Where you off to?" Lou asks.

"I think I'm going to pay old Herm a little visit."

"What for?"

"I just want to poke the bear a little bit."

There's a little old white-haired lady leaning on a cane, toting a large basket down the street. I recognize her from the meeting at the church. She was the one all fired up to fight.

I tip my hat. "Can I help you with that basket, ma'am?"

"It's not ma'am, it's Elvira," she says, peering up at me. "Ma'am's short for madam you know, and I'm sure as dickens not one of those."

No, I didn't know that. I can't imagine what difference it makes, but I leave it alone.

"And I don't need help with the basket either." It sure looks like she does, the way she's bent clear over trying to keep it off the ground. "I don't blame you for asking, but once I start taking help, where does it stop? With me in a pine box, that's where."

"Well, then, I'll be on my way."

I start to turn away, but she stops me, grabbing onto my forearm with surprising strength. "You remember what I said, sonny. Remember."

"About what?"

"About fighting. I can help. Look." She sets the basket down in the street and pulls back the cloth covering it. There's four chickens in there, staring up at me. She reaches down in among them and pulls out an old black powder pistol.

"My late husband, god damn his soul, taught me to shoot. He was a worthless shit, but he knew how to shoot." She has the tip of her tongue caught in her teeth and she peers around, looking for something to shoot to prove it to me. The gun is a giant, heavy thing and it weaves dangerously in her grip.

"I believe you," I say quickly, pushing the gun barrel down. Just in time too, because she squeezes the trigger right then and with a huge bang and a cloud of smoke it goes off, the ball digging a little trench in the street.

"Now you made me miss!" she snaps.

A good thing too. She was pointing it at someone's house. Right then the door opens and an old man comes charging out. He's not dressed yet, wearing nothing but long underwear. His white hair is sticking out in all directions.

"I told you to stop carrying that gun around, Elvira!" he shouts. "You're going to kill someone one of these days and it might be me!"

"Oh, just rein in your horses, Elmer!" she shouts back. "I know what I'm doing!"

"Sheriff, you need to arrest that woman. She's a menace is what she is."

"You'd have your own wife arrested?" she shrieks, bringing the gun up and working on cocking it. "I'll learn you a lesson, I will."

I wrestle the gun away from her before she can do any more harm.

"Now you're taking *his* side?" she hollers.

"I'm not taking anyone's side. I'm trying to keep people from getting killed."

"I was just going to wing him," she pouts.

"I thought you said your husband was dead."

"He *is* dead. Both my first two are dead. That there is my third husband, only we don't live together anymore."

"That's because you're an evil she-demon!" he yells.

Elvira starts grabbing for the pistol again. "Just one shot," she says. "I'll teach him to speak to a lady that way."

I hold the pistol up where she can't reach it. "Why don't you come by my office later and pick it up? After you cool off?"

They're both shouting at me as I walk away. I wonder if this is the sort of thing sheriffs have to put up with often.

I put the old lady's gun in my desk drawer and go on over to the bank. Herm is sitting behind his desk. He looks up when the door opens, a smile on his face. Then he sees it's me and he lets the smile go.

"What do you want?"

"I thought I'd open a bank account. I've never had one before. Maybe it's time to start."

"You don't have any money."

"Not true." I pull out the last few dollars of what Lou paid me. "I have this."

"That's not enough to open an account. You have to have at least ten dollars."

I give him my best innocent look. "Soon I'll have a thousand. Will that be enough?"

"Har, har," he says. "Very funny."

"What was that noise you just made?"

"What?"

222222222

"That noise? 'Har, har.' What does that mean?"

He frowns at me. "Are you pulling my leg?"

"Nope."

"It was a fake laugh. To show you what I think of your thousand dollars." He leans forward and puts his beefy forearms on the desk. "Get it through your thick head, Injun. You're not ever going to collect that money. If it even exists. Which any fool would want to make sure of before he gets himself killed over it."

"How much?" I ask him.

He looks puzzled. "How much what?"

"How much money are you willing to get killed over?"

His eyes get real big and he shoots a look at the safe. "If you're thinking about robbing the bank you can disabuse yourself of that notion right now. That's a Hammerstein safe and—"

"I know, I know. Hammerstein safes are the best. You can throw them off a cliff and drown them in a beaver pond and they won't break open. I'm not here to rob you."

I pull my duster back and show him my star. I'm actually quite proud of it. I polish it every day and it shines. "I'm the sheriff, remember?"

"You're a drifter, that's what you are."

"There's no need to get snappy," I tell him.

"You come in here and threaten me..."

"Mister, I haven't threatened you yet. When I do, you'll know it. Now, answer my question. How much money are you willing to get killed over?"

His eyes dart around, trying to see where I'm going. It makes him look like a ferret. "Only a fool gets himself killed over money."

"I agree." I put my hands on his desk and lean forward so he can see my eyes real clear. "*This* is the part where I threaten you. I know who you are and I know what you're doing and I want you to listen to something and make sure you hear it just right. These are good folks in this town and I'm fond of them. I don't want to see bad things happen to them."

"What are you insinuating? I know they're good folks. If anything, I'm guilty of caring too much about them. I don't want to see any of them get hurt." He's trying to bluster, but there's sweat on his upper lip. His eyes dart to my guns.

"Good. Then we agree on something else." I pull back and stand upright. I put my hand on the butt of my gun. "If a single one of them gets hurt, I'm holding you accountable. I'll find you, it doesn't matter how far you run, and I'll kill you. Do you understand me?"

He licks his lips. The first time he tries, he can't get any words out. When he does get something out, his voice is dry and scratchy. "I…I understand."

"Good. Then you won't need to take any more late night rides in the dark. You can sleep safe and sound in your bed like an honest citizen, knowing Sheriff Ace is on the job, protecting you."

I tip my hat and walk out the door.

33

I head on over to the boarding house near midday and drop down in my regular seat. Pearl comes out of the kitchen when she hears the door close and smiles real big at me. I can smell fresh bread and that means she's been baking. I'm not sure there's a thing in this world that smells better than fresh bread.

"Almost time for your date with Annie," she says.

I wince. The truth is I've been getting sweaty palms all day whenever I think about it.

"You're not going to wear that shirt, are you?"

I look down at my shirt. Sure, it's more brown than white, but... It *did* used to be white, didn't it? When I first bought it? I pull my duster closed and look up at Pearl. "What's wrong with my shirt?"

"I'd call it disreputable, but that's only because I'm too much of a lady to say what I really think of it."

"I've never known you to hold back from saying what you really think about something."

"True enough." She shakes a finger at me. "If you show up wearing that dirty old rag, you'll be lucky if she lets you in the door. And then there's no chance you'll get any of this." She leers at me and makes a rude gesture in the air.

I feel my face get hot. "Why'd you have to go and do that, Pearl?" I protest. "It's not like that."

"Don't whitewash me, Ace. You're a young buck and she's a young doe. It's *always* like that."

"We're just friends."

"If that's all you are, then why'd your face turn so red?"

"Because...Apache?"

"Pish. Don't hide behind that redskin malarkey. Your face turned red because you're embarrassed and you're embarrassed because you favor Annie. Don't deny it. Ain't no shame in that."

"Am I going to get any food?"

"You'll get food when we're done conversating here. Now, since you never answered my first question I'm going to take it to mean you do intend to wear that foul thing on your date. Probably because you don't have another one, right?"

"I have another shirt." She fixes me with her strongest look and I shift in my chair. "Sort of. But this is my nice one."

"I knew it. You know, you'd be a fine looking man if you'd just take a bit of care." She takes my chin in her hand and turns my face side to side, studying me like I'm a horse she's thinking of buying. "It's a shame about the lack of a proper beard, or at least a mustache, but I've heard some women don't like them anyway."

Having no beard or mustache does make me stick out a bit, I've noticed. But in this area my Apache blood wins out. I can't grow more than the faintest stubble on my face.

She lets go of my face and disappears. A minute later she's back and she's holding up a man's shirt. "It's not much, but it's clean," she says.

"Where'd you get that?"

"When I heard about your date yesterday I went to see Ancil. It's one of his."

Now I really feel dumb. Probably the whole town's laughing at the poor half-breed who can't even afford a proper shirt.

"Wipe that look off your face, Ace. I can see you're thinking about refusing and I won't have it. Ancil done you a neighborly thing and you're going to up and accept it. Stand up so I can see how this fits on you."

With a sigh I stand up. She holds the shirt up against me. "Hmm. I'll have to take it in a bit here around the middle, but otherwise it should hold up. You make sure you're here about an hour before. I'll dig out the old copper tub and heat some water."

"A bath?"

"Try not to sound like a little kid made to wash behind his ears, Ace. It won't endear you to Annie. Trust me on this."

"I was thinking of dunking myself in the creek…"

She shakes her head. "There's no substitute for hot water and soap."

I don't bother arguing anymore. Pearl's like a pie-eyed gelding with the bit in his teeth. She won't let go. It's easier just to give in.

"While you're off on your date I'll wash that rag you call a shirt. Or burn it. Whichever is easier."

"You're not burning my favorite shirt."

"Of course not, sweetie." She pinches my cheek. "Just trying to get a rise out of you. Don't expect I'll be the only woman today to get a rise out of you, will I?"

It takes me a moment to realize what she's saying and when I do my cheeks get all hot again. Pearl busts out laughing and heads into the kitchen.

34

After I eat, I climb back on Coyote and head out of town. From her seat on the porch of the sheriff's office—sitting in *my* chair of course—Lou waves me down.

"So even after I advised you against it, you went and had a talk with Herm. Don't deny it. I saw his face earlier."

"Herm and I had a right nice talk. I think we're going to be friends now."

She looks up at me and shakes her head. "If I didn't know better, I'd think you was one of those fellers that likes to poke a stick in a hornet's nest and see them get mad."

"Only when the hornets deserve it."

"You get stung much in that line of work?"

"Sometimes." I nod toward her shotgun, which is leaning against the wall next to her. "Say, you and Betsy have any plans tonight?"

"I thought you and young Annie had a date." She grins real big at me.

I sigh. Between Pearl and Lou I'm starting to have second thoughts about this. "It's after that."

"You think we'll have uninvited guests tonight?"

"There's no way to tell for sure, but it's best to be ready."

"Well I'd planned on paying a little visit to Virgil tonight, but it can wait I guess."

"You and Virgil are getting pretty chummy." I try my best to give her one of the looks she and Pearl have been giving me, suggesting all kinds of lewd things without saying them out loud.

Lou scowls. "What's wrong with you, Ace? You've *seen* Virgil, right?"

I wink at her. "There's no need to be shy about it."

"I'm done humoring you on this. You and I both know Virgil's crazy as a bag of rats and we both also know he's the only one with any liquor in this town."

"So it's funny when *you* do it, but not when I do."

"Something like that."

I ride on out. On the way I see that someone is building a barn next to his house. There's a group of men gathered around. I ride over closer.

It's a barn raising. The walls of the barn have all been built and are lying on the ground. One of them has ropes attached to it and it looks like they're fixing to throw their backs into it.

"You men need any help?" I ask.

There's a chorus of "Good afternoon, Sheriff Ace" and lots of smiles. Ancil breaks off from the rest and comes over. He pushes his flat-brimmed straw hat back and wipes his forehead.

"We'd be obliged for your help, Sheriff Ace, but we don't want to take you away from your duties."

"It's no trouble. I have time. I'm surprised though."

"By what?"

"Most folks wouldn't build a new barn at a time like this, what with the troubles and all."

"We were doubtful, it's true," he says. "But that was before you showed up. We're confident you'll take care of this little problem for us." The others nod and smile.

"I appreciate your confidence, but I'm just one man. A whole pack of things could go wrong."

"One man with the power of the Lord behind him," Ancil says, holding up one finger like I'm a little kid who forgot his lesson.

"What makes you say that?"

"You came in our time of need. Clearly you were sent by Him."

I have nothing to say to that so I decide to let it be. "Why don't you hand me one of those ropes. I'll take a dally around my saddlehorn and Coyote will be happy to help lift those walls into place."

Coyote turns his head and gives me a hard eye. He's letting me know that whatever he is, it isn't happy.

"Be neighborly, Coyote. They need our help."

I don't think that makes him any happier, but we set to and help those men out and he doesn't kick or bite anyone so I take that as a good sign.

When we're done we ride out and head toward the Hashknife spread. A few miles out of town there's a little rocky peak. I'm able to ride most of the way to the top, then I hop down and make the rest of the way on foot.

As I thought, from there I'm able to see all the way to the Hashknife headquarters through my looking glass. I check the land pretty thoroughly but don't see any sign of approaching riders. What I do see is quite a few cowboys out gathering cattle and starting to head them toward headquarters.

That means roundup is coming. That gives me the ghost of an idea. I'm still not sure what to do with it, so I push it to the back of my mind and let it rest for now.

On my way back to town I come across Virgil. He's stripped down to just his britches and is splashing around in the creek with a funny looking spear in his hand. I ride up on him and call out, ask him what in the blazes he's doing.

He looks at me like I just said I was the queen of England. "You playing with me? Any durned fool can see I'm froggin'."

"You're what?" His exposed skin is unbelievably white and looks strange against the leathery color of his face, neck and hands. He's painfully skinny too, with this little pot belly that sticks out pretty far.

"I'm froggin'." He frowns at me. "You telling me you never et frog legs before?"

"I don't believe I have."

"You're missing out. There's nothing better."

I think about how small frog legs are. "You're going to need a lot of them."

He points to a gunny sack lying on the bank. "I'm working on it. Now go away, you're scaring off the frogs."

"Before I do, I need to ask your help."

He squints up at me. "What fer?"

"Could be we'll have some varmints show up to town tonight, looking for trouble. I wonder if you and your squirrel gun would like to help run them off."

He smiles and shows off his scraggly tooth. "Why that's right nice of you, Ace. Now I got something to look forward to all day."

131

"Be at the church an hour or so after dark."

35

I hate to admit it, but the bath isn't so bad. It's even kind of nice. The bad part is when I'm soaking in the tub and Pearl comes bustling in with another kettle of hot water to pour in.

"Pearl!" I yelp.

"Pish," she says, dumping the boiling water in the tub. "Not like it's something I haven't seen before."

"Just go away."

"Okay, okay." She stops in the doorway. "I want you to know something, Ace. I really appreciate what you're doing here. And if there's anything I can do to help, I mean anything, like picking up a rifle and doing some shooting of my own, I will."

"I'll remember that."

"They're good folks here in Lily Creek. The best folks. The kind who take you in and treat you like one of their own. The kind who don't judge you, no matter what you had to do to survive."

She sounds different all of a sudden. Kind of misty and sad, but not the bad kind of sad. I don't know how to describe it.

"You want to know what I did before this?" she asks.

"You don't have to tell me."

She tosses her hair. "No. I want to. Not because I'm proud of what I done, but so's you know what kind of people these are. See, I was a saloon girl in Dodge City before this. Three years of sweaty, ruttin' cowboys. Three years of pouring as much whiskey as I could down my throat trying to burn it all away."

She slumps down in a chair then and puts her head in her hands. When she looks up at me there's tears in her eyes.

"What was I supposed to do? My husband, Carl, and I came West to start a new life. But someone shot Carl and he died and I was left all alone. I didn't have any money. There weren't any jobs. I couldn't leave. I didn't want to starve."

She wipes her eyes and stands up. "Ancil came through town, on his way home to Lily Creek. He saw me crying my eyes out one morning on the front step of the saloon. I figured he was just like everyone else. See, when you're a saloon girl there's two types of men. The ones who want to use you and the ones who condemn you.

"But Ancil wasn't either. He just held out his hand and said, 'You want out?'" She has to stop and wipe at her eyes again.

"He brought me here with him. No one said a word against me. They just took me in. They helped me build this place and start a new life." She gets a grim, serious look on her face. "You have to stop Dace Jackson, Ace. You have to make sure he doesn't steal this land from them. Promise me that."

"I'll do what I can, Pearl."

"I need more than that."

"I'll stop them. I won't let them take Lily Creek. I promise you that."

She nods and some of the worry leaves her face. "Thank you. Now hurry up and finish your bath. You don't want to be late for your date, do you?"

I wince. There's that word again.

Twenty minutes later I'm ready to go. My hair's still wet, but there's nothing I can do about that. I'm a whole lot cleaner, that's for sure. While I was in the bath, Pearl somehow managed to get the worst of the dirt out of my hat, though there was nothing she could do about the holes. She also shined my boots.

I feel as bright and clean as a new penny.

"Wait," Pearl calls out as I'm reaching for the door. I turn back.

Pearl snatches the flowers out of one of the vases and hands them to me.

I'm puzzled. "What are these?"

"They're flowers. Surely you know what flowers are."

"Yes, I know what flowers are. But what are they for?"

"To give to Annie."

"Why?"

"Darn it, Ace, are you *trying* to be difficult? You're giving them to her because women like men to bring them flowers when they're courting them."

My mouth goes dry. "*Courting?*"

"Enough talking. Just go already." She shoves me out the door and closes it behind me.

I stand there on the stoop, unable to move. I still can't believe it. Did she say *courting*? Isn't courting something you do when you're fixing to marry someone?

I can't get married. I have too many places to go.

Why would someone like Annie want to marry someone like me anyway? I'm a half-breed drifter. Like as not I'll get myself killed in the next few days.

I walk down the street. Everyone's watching me, I'm sure of it. I can't see them, but I can feel them looking through their curtains, peeking out their windows.

What have I gotten myself into?

36

Somehow I make it to Annie's, though I'm as skittish as a new colt by the time I get there. I lift my hand to knock on the door and it's shaking. I take a couple deep breaths and try to calm down, remember who I am. Ace Lone Wolf, remember? I faced an Aztec god and survived. How hard can this be?

But it doesn't help. I still feel as weak in the knees as a newborn calf.

I raise my hand again, but before I can knock, she opens the door.

She looks lovely. She's brushed her hair until it shines. She's wearing this peach-colored dress that makes her skin look as soft as dew.

"Hello, Ace," she says.

I open my mouth. Nothing. Maybe a couple choking sounds, but no actual words. I try to swallow but I can't even do that.

She smiles and it's so bright it almost hurts. "What's the matter, Ace? Cat got your tongue?"

Something's got it, that's for sure.

Her eyes fall on the flowers in my hand. "Are those for me?"

I look down. I'd honestly forgotten I was holding them. They look a little crumpled, like maybe I held them too tight. I hold them out to her. My first word emerges.

"Here."

"Why thank you, Ace. They're lovely." She tries to take them, but I'm still holding on tight. "I think you're supposed to let go of them."

"Oh. Sorry."

I wince. Why did I have to go and say that? I sound like an idiot.

She holds the flowers up and smells them. "How sweet of you." She steps aside. "Won't you come in?"

What I want to do is run.

"Come on. I won't bite." She takes my hand and pulls me inside.

The first thing I see is two little heads poking around the corner from the door to the next room, wide eyes staring at me.

"Don't be rude, children. Come out and say hi to Ace."

They come spilling into the room in a rush.

"Ace is here!"

"Hi, Ace!"

They run and grab onto my legs. Somehow having them there helps ease my nerves a little. I pat them on the head.

Camila looks up at me. "Can I ask you something, Ace?"

"Sure."

"You're too tall. Come down close where I can see you."

I crouch down to her level. She puts her little hands on my cheeks and looks into my eyes. What she says next floors me.

"Are you courtin' Mama?"

"Am I...*what*?"

"It's a simple question. Are you—"

"I heard the question the first time," I say, cutting her off before she can finish. I don't need to hear that word again right now. I look up and see Annie is standing there with her hand over her mouth, trying not to laugh, and that makes it worse.

"I'm sorry," Annie says. "It's rude of me to laugh. But you should have seen the look on your face just then."

To Camila she says, "I already told you children. I'm just having Ace over to dinner. Don't make this so hard on the poor man."

"I was only asking," Camila says, putting her little fist on her hip. "I got a right to know."

"It's 'I *have* a right to know,'" Annie replied. "Don't say got. It makes you sound uneducated. And no, you don't have a right to know. It's none of your beeswax. You children have said hello, now get along to your room and get ready for bed."

Camila's lower lip sticks out like it does when she gets stubborn. "I'm not tired."

Diego echoes her and runs around the room a couple times to prove it.

They're in bed a few minutes later and Annie comes out and closes the door behind her. "Oh good, you're still here. I thought you might have run off. I hope you're hungry, because I made a lot."

I'm not sure I am hungry. Mostly I want a nice tall glass of whiskey.

But when the food comes I realize that I actually am hungry. Top notch chili and hot cornbread fresh out of the oven. Corn and real butter on the side.

"There's pie if you save room."

Now I'm hoping I was wrong about those men from the Hashknife showing up tonight. I'm going to need to sleep this food off like a hibernating bear.

An hour later, so full I think I'll have to roll out the door when I leave, Annie brings us each a cup of coffee. Before she can sit down there's a ruckus from the children's room and she excuses herself and goes in there. A couple minutes later she's back at the table.

"They wear me out, those children do. They're a real handful." She sits back down. "No doubt you've been wondering about us, me raising them with no husband and them not looking much like me."

"It's crossed my mind, but I figured you'd tell me if you wanted to. If not, that's okay too."

She gets a sad look on her face. "I do want to tell you. I came out here from Ohio in a wagon with my parents and a few other families. In Denver we turned south and split off from the others. Outside of Santa Fe we ran into a Mexican family who was heading for the Arizona Territory and we joined up with them.

"It was late in the year. We should have just stayed in Santa Fe until spring. But my father thought we could make it. He wanted to get out and stake our homestead. He wanted an early jump on planting the spring crops, said if we waited in Santa Fe it'd be too late to get decent crops in the ground.

"We were deep in the mountains when the blizzard struck." Her voice chokes off and she brushes at a tear. "We had no choice but to hole up and try to ride it out. The storm lasted four days and when it was done the snow was in drifts over my head. It was awful. There was no chance we could go on.

"We did what we could. We built a rough shelter and kept a fire going, prayed for a miracle. But there was no miracle. The oxen died first, then the horses. They plain froze to death. We ate the animals. Somehow we eked by. The men made makeshift snowshoes and we made plans to walk out.

"But more storms followed and by the time they passed, Maria, the children's mother, was too weak to walk. My mother wasn't too much better. Pedro, Maria's husband, headed out during a lull in the storms to bring help, but he never returned.

"Maria died in January. Mother in early February. At least I think it was February. It was hard to be sure." Her tears are flowing freely now but she makes no move to brush them away. There's so much pain in her voice and my heart aches with it. I wish so badly that I could do something, but I can't.

"Father did everything he could. He hunted. He gathered wood. He fixed our shelter when the snow collapsed it. I watched him grow weaker and weaker. I knew what he was doing, how he was giving me and the little ones most of the food, but when I tried to get him to take more, he refused. He blamed himself for what was happening and he tried to make it right.

"He died near the end of the winter. Shortly after that the weather started to break. The sun came out and I knew it was then or never. We had some deer meat that Father had shot. I packed it up and we bundled up in every stitch of clothing we had and we struck out.

"By the time we hit Lily Creek we were nearly dead. I was carrying both of them—they were little things, just two and three at the time—and I could only go a dozen steps at a time before I had to stop and rest.

"It was Amos and Raphaela who found us and brought us in. Come spring everyone pitched in and built us this house, gave us seeds, helped us get a garden going." Now she wipes away her tears, using her apron. "We've been a family ever since."

I don't know what to say. The strength in this young woman, what she's done, what she's doing. She reminds me of my own mother, and what she went through to get our clan safely to Pah-Gotzin-Kay.

Annie pulls her chair a little closer to me and leans over and puts her hand on my arm, just for a moment, then takes it off.

"I hope you won't think me too forward, Ace but..." She trails off, suddenly unsure.

"It's okay. I could never think anything bad about you, Annie." And I mean it too. I don't know if the angels I've heard people talk about are real, but if they are, Annie's probably one.

"I've learned the hard way that things can change really fast out here. It's a rough land and it can be unforgiving. A person can't be too hesitant, lest something valuable be taken away and it's too late.

"I don't know what's going to happen next. Dace Jackson is a bad man and he has a lot of bad men working for him."

Now I cut in. "Don't you worry, Annie. I'll take care of them."

She smiles and touches my arm again. "And I have a great deal of confidence in you, Ace. But I also know how fast bad things can happen. That's why I'm going to be forward here.

This time she takes my hand. A big old lump suddenly appears in my throat. I stare at her hand like a bird staring at a snake. I'm completely frozen.

"You're a good man, Ace. One of the best. What you're doing for this town, the way you are with the children. I just...I want you to know that I have the highest esteem for you." She frowns, real pretty like. "That didn't come out right. No, what I mean is that I like you, Ace. I really like you. You're the kind of man who doesn't come along too often."

She lets go of my hand and leans back. "I don't know what's going to come next, but I wanted you to know that. I wanted to say it in case...in case I didn't get a chance to later."

I want to tell her that I feel the same way. For some reason I've got the words for it and everything. But before I can start I hear kissing noises and giggling coming from the children's room. They've got their door partway open and they're peeking out at us.

"You're supposed to be in bed!" Annie jumps up and heads for them. They slam the door and I hear running feet.

Annie turns back. "I'm sorry about that, Ace," but she's laughing like I am.

"They're kids," I say. I get up. "I need to be going now anyway."

"So soon?"

It's been dark for an hour at least. Lou and Virgil should be waiting by the church. Besides, I need some time to grapple with what she's said, what it means to me.

"I have to patrol. I think they're going to try something tonight."

She follows me to the door. When I go to tip my hat, she surprises me by giving me a quick hug. "Stay safe, okay?"

I walk out into the night thinking I never had so much reason to stay safe before.

37

Lou and Virgil are waiting at the church, passing a flask between them.

"Time for the fun to start," Virgil says, waving his rifle over his head and hooting.

"You shouldn't be needing that tonight," I tell him. "Not for what I have planned."

"Well, dagnabbit! What did I come for anyhow if I can't shoot anyone?"

"Don't let it get you down. If this doesn't go like I planned, you'll get your chance."

That cheers him up. He settles down and takes another swig off the flask. "What's the plan?"

When I'm done telling them there's silence while both of them think about it. Lou speaks first. "What makes you think they'll hit the church first?"

"It's out at the edge of town, for one. For another, it's the church. It's important to the people here. If the plan is to drive them off, what better place to start than the church?"

Virgil takes off his coonskin hat and scratches his bald head. "Makes sense to me."

"Dammit, Virgil," Lou growls. "What did I tell you about taking your hat off? It smells like you're hiding a dead rat under there. Put it back on."

I asked around earlier and borrowed a ladder and a couple big buckets, which I filled with water. Now we set the ladder up and they climb up onto the roof of the church with the buckets.

"I don't know why we got to go to all this trouble," Virgil complains. "I still say it would be better if we just shot 'em and was done with it."

"If we go shooting too many people we'll end up with the governor involved and he'll send the Arizona Rangers. We don't want that."

"We could shoot them too," Virgil says hopefully.

"Virgil. Promise me you're not going to shoot anyone unless you have to."

He grumbles to himself.

"Virgil!"

"What does 'have to' mean? Like, when I got an itch and I just have to scratch it?"

"I'm going to send you home, Virgil," I say sternly.

"All right, no need to git in a snit. I won't shoot anyone less'n they sorely need shooting."

I figure that's the best I'm going to get. "Stay quiet," I tell them.

I whistle and Coyote comes trotting up. He's got no saddle or bridle on, but I can get by without them. I can guide him with my knees and I don't want to risk the extra noise that a saddle and bridle make. I've ditched my boots and I'm wearing my moccasins.

We head on out of town, following the road that leads to the Hashknife spread. Then we melt into the bushes and settle down to wait. I hope Wilkins doesn't make me wait too long. I don't want Virgil and Lou getting too drunk up there on the roof. No telling what Virgil will do once he's good and liquored up.

Sitting there waiting turns out to be harder than it should be. I can't stop thinking about Annie. My mind just runs on and on about her, like a runaway chicken that won't come back to the coop. Part of me is jumping up and down that she likes me, but a whole lot of me is shaking afraid and wants to light out. Could I really settle down with her? Raise kids? Live amongst the white man for the rest of my life? What about my mother and my clan, back in Pah-Gotzin-Kay?

It's a relief when I hear riders approaching. My eyes have fully adjusted to the darkness and I count six of them, which is about what I expected. This is a raid, not a full assault on the town. They're planning on burning a few buildings and when I come out to stop them, shooting me down. To their thinking six men should have no trouble handling one.

I'm about to prove them wrong.

They pass by me and I follow. So long as no one looks over his shoulder, they won't see me back here and they sure won't hear me. Coyote is as quiet as a deer anyway and I tied rags around his feet to further muffle the sound of his hooves. If there's one thing we Apaches know, it's nighttime raids.

For men who think they're being quiet, the six of them are making a lot of racket. The creaking of their saddles, the jingle of spurs, it all carries in the quiet night air. It makes me feel better about the chances that my plan will work.

Of course, once I stop them tonight they'll only try something else, and something else. Sooner or later they're bound to get through. Maybe Virgil is right. Maybe we should just shoot as many as we can whenever we can.

But my gut tells me that's a bad idea. A man like Dace Jackson is bound to have powerful friends. Right now he's keeping this all under the blanket, trying not to draw any notice. We start killing his men he might call on those friends. Better to avoid that.

So I try not to think about what comes next. Thinking about the future makes a man careless in the present, and that gets you killed.

About fifty yards from the church they leave the road and ride into some trees. I slide off Coyote, give him a pat on the butt, and soft foot it after them. They're tying their horses to the trees and talking in low voices.

"Give me one of them torches," a man says. Sounds like Wilkins. That cheers me up. Maybe there'll be a need to shoot him. I sure wouldn't lose any sleep over it.

When the man with the torches tied to his saddle doesn't come up with them right away, Wilkins gets impatient. "Come on, get a wiggle on. We ain't got all night."

Finally the man gets the knot loose. Torches are passed out to all the men and I smell the sharp odor of kerosene as they pour it on the torches.

"No more talking," Wilkins says, and leads them out of the trees toward the church.

As soon as they're gone I draw my knife and pay a visit to their horses. Make a few quick strategic cuts and then I follow them.

They gather up beside the church. I creep on until I get around the corner of the church, and peek out at them.

"Who's got the matches?"

"I thought you brought 'em."

Wilkins starts swearing, calling the lot of them all kinds of names they don't seem too happy about.

Finally one of them says, "Hang on. I found 'em. No, just one."

"What the hell are you doing with just one match?" Wilkins hisses.

"Hobble your lip," the man snaps back. "Got a hole in my pocket. The rest musta fell out."

"What kind of purblind fool puts the matches in a pocket with a hole in it?"

"The kind who's thinking about putting a hole in you," the man growls back.

"Just light the damn thing already and let's get this done," another man says.

They all gather in a tight circle, holding the torches close together. There's a spark, then a flare as the man with the match lights it. He cups it with his free hand and holds it up close to the torches. I want them blinded by the sudden light so I wait for the torches to flare up before I call out.

"Now!"

Lou and Virgil rise up on the roof and dump the buckets of water on the knot of men. They're big buckets, close to five gallons each, and it puts a pretty good soaking on them. The torches sputter and go out.

A second later Lou and Virgil start shooting into the air and hollering bloody murder. I told them to make it sound like there was a lot of them and they're doing a fine job of it.

Confused, wet, surprised, the men take off running for their horses. They fire off a few shots as they go, but they don't bother to aim, just firing into the darkness.

I whistle and Coyote comes trotting up. I jump on and we circle around the men, getting on the far side of them. A minute later here they come boiling out of the trees and there I am waiting in the middle of the road.

"You boys looking for me?" I yell. Then Coyote and I take off at a gallop.

Howling and cursing, they come after me, like I figured they would. They start shooting, but they're still not seeing too good so their shots go wild. I make it harder by cutting side to side, dodging around as much as I can.

As I ride, I'm waiting for what I know is coming.

Any second now.

They're splashing across the creek when the first cinch I cut gives way. One moment the saddle is in place on the horse's back, and the next it isn't. It just slides right off the horse's back. With a yelp, the rider goes tumbling into the water. His horse bolts.

"What the...?" one of them yells. "What just happened to Lem?"

The same thing that's about to happen to you.

The next cinch breaks and the rider goes head over heels off the back of his horse and thumps on the ground.

One by one the others suffer the same fate, while everyone looks around trying to figure out what's happening.

Once they're all down I circle back around. I take my time to give them a chance to gather up. I hear plenty of cursing and vows of terrible vengeance when I get close. It all makes me smile.

I slide off Coyote and take cover behind a fallen tree.

"Forget to tighten your cinches, boys?" I call out. They spin toward me and a dozen bullets come my way, but none even get close.

"You're just wasting lead, you know that? I've got cover and I've got a clean line of fire." A few more shots ring out.

"Spread out," Wilkins says. "We'll flank him."

When they start to move I put a couple of shots real close to them, to sort of change their minds. "Are you boys simple? Did you not understand what it meant when I said I have cover, a line of fire? The next one who moves is getting shot."

That settles them down.

"That's better. You stay calm, you can still walk out of here. You start acting crazy, I'll have no choice but to shoot you."

"You ain't gonna kill us all," Wilkins says.

"I'd like not to. See, here's what I'm thinking. I'm thinking some of you are just hired hands. You're not gunslingers, you're cowboys. Am I right?"

There's a few mumbles.

"How much are they paying you? Thirty dollars a month? Forty? Is that enough to get killed over?"

That starts them thinking. One of them says, "I'm only getting thirty-five." A couple more agree with him.

"Don't listen to him," Wilkins says. "He's a lyin' Injun. He don't know what he's talking about."

I put a bullet right between his feet. He yelps and jumps.

"I could just as easy have put that in your gut, Wilkins," I say. "Or you think I'm lying about that too?"

"Why don't you come out and face me like a man?"

I sigh. "I'd like nothing better. I've been itching to shoot you for some time now. But I'm the law now. I'm trying to do things the right way.

"The rest of you listen to me. I'm giving you this one chance. Drag your freight and light out. I won't go easy on you again. Next time I see a one of you within spitting distance of Lily Creek I'll kill you. You have my word on that. Take some friendly advice. You're bucking a stacked deck. It's your call."

"Don't listen to him," Wilkins snaps. "He's only one man."

"Not for long I'm not. We sent a rider to Phoenix. He should be getting there tomorrow. He's going to meet with the governor and tell him what's going on here. In two days the Arizona Rangers will be heading this way and the lot of you are going to hang."

Sure, I made it all up, but it sounds good. And it gets them thinking. Wilkins starts to bluster but one of them tells him to shut up.

"I didn't sign up for this," he says. "I'm drawing my pay and cutting out."

He starts walking away. One by one the others follow until only Wilkins is left.

"This ain't over," he says. "Not by a far piece. Buford sent out the word, put a lot of money on your head. There's some real gunslicks coming. You ever hear of John Wesley Hardin? How about James Miller? The one they call Killin' Jim?"

That makes my blood run cold. They're two of the most feared gunmen in the West.

"When they get here, they're going to gun you down like a dog. You hear?"

"I hear you, Wilkins. I do enjoy our little chats. Next time be sure to give me a reason to shoot you, okay?"

He walks away and I stand there and wonder what I'm going to do next.

38

In the morning I head over to Ancil's blacksmith shop. "I want you to spread the word. They're going to get serious now."

He sets his hammer down. His face is grim. "I heard they tried to burn the church down. That sounds serious to me."

"It's not. Tell everyone to keep their children close. Be ready to get indoors and bolt the doors. Keep their heads down."

"We'll set up a rotation, have someone ready on the church bell. When trouble comes they can ring the bell and warn everyone."

I hadn't thought of that. "Be good if you could have someone up in the tower at all times, keeping watch. I can't be everywhere at once." I hesitate. I'm not sure how he'll take what I say next. Will he think I'm abandoning them?

"I have to leave for a couple days. Lou and Virgil will be here, but that's it."

He nods. "Okay."

That surprises me. "Aren't you going to ask where I'm going, why I'm leaving you right now?"

"Nope. I trust you, Ace. If you say you have to go, then I know it's important."

That staggers me. This man barely knows me and yet he's willing to trust me this much?

I look down, realize I'm still wearing his shirt. I put it on this morning without thinking about it. "I'll get this back to you as soon as I can get over to Pearl's and change."

He waves me off. "Keep it. It's little enough, next to what you're doing for us."

"Pearl speaks highly of you."

"She's quite a woman."

"You should tell her that."

He looks at me for a moment, then nods. "Aye. I probably should."

At Pearl's I change into my old shirt and grab my gear. When I head for the door, Pearl is already there holding a cloth sack.

"It's enough for a few days," she says, handing it to me. "The bread is fresh this morning."

"Aren't you going to ask me either?"

"I can see you're a man in a hurry. It won't be me who slows you down." There's something else she wants to say. I can see it in her eyes.

"What is it?"

"Speak to Annie before you leave. A woman has that right."

I start to tell her that I was already planning on it, then realize that it's not true. I'm confused when it comes to Annie. Part of me is looking forward to the long hours in the saddle when I can hopefully wrestle it out.

I tie my gear on the saddle and mount up. Lou is sitting out front of the sheriff's office. I toss her my badge. "You're sheriff for the next couple of days. Try to keep Virgil from shooting anyone."

"You're fetching help, I hope."

"There's just the three of us."

"Going to find the old gang?"

That surprises me. "I keep forgetting how smart you are, you hide it so well."

She spits a stream of tobacco juice and wipes her chin. "I could say the same about you."

"We need more hands."

"What about that Boyce feller? There's bad blood between you, right?"

"Settling up with Boyce is just an added benefit."

"See that you come back in one piece."

"I will."

She snorts. "Maybe. Unless he gets lucky. If you're smart, you'll bushwhack him, take the guesswork out of it."

"I can't do that."

She shakes her head. "He set you up to hang and still you say that. All these years I been a man, and I still get surprised at how dumb men can be. Learn to think like a woman. You'll live longer."

"They're sending gunfighters next. Real gunslicks, high-dollar killers. But I reckon it will take them a few days at least to get here. That's why I have to go now. If those men kill me, I want someone here to help protect the town."

"Ride fast."

Next I go to Annie's. She's out front, planting some flowers in her yard, She looks up and knows right away I'm leaving. I climb down off Coyote and she hurries over to me and takes my hands before I can speak.

"You be safe now, you hear?" Her voice cracks as she speaks and I get a tightness in my throat to hear it. "There's someone here who wants you back in one piece."

"I don't get it, Annie. I'm just a no-account drifter. None of you knew I existed before a few days ago, but everyone, Ancil, Pearl, now you, you're all so trusting. How is that?"

"Maybe it's your thinking that's wrong. Maybe you need to stop thinking of yourself as a no-account drifter and start thinking of yourself as just a man. A good man. That's how we think of you."

Now my throat's gone and closed up completely. I hope by whatever gods there are that she doesn't start crying because I'm afraid I will too.

She gives me a hug and squeezes me tight. She feels fragile as a bird in my arms, but strong too. She's got sand, this woman has.

She pulls back. "Whatever it takes, you come back to me safe, you hear?"

"I aim to." I climb on Coyote.

The children come out and wave as I ride away.

39

It's not that hard to find their hideout. I go back to where they tried to hold up the wagon and start from there. Their tracks have faded a lot, but I learned tracking from my grandfather, the great Apache chief Cochise, and I'm able to pick up their trail after a few minutes.

The trail leads me deeper into the mountains. It follows a little stream up through the aspens, across open, grassy meadows and finally into a dense stand of pine trees. When I come out the other side of the pine trees I see an area of granite dells up ahead, huge outcroppings of lichen-spattered granite rocks in a hilly area.

I stop in the shadow of the trees and consider my options. They're almost surely back in those rocks. It's a pretty good place to defend, which means Boyce isn't a complete idiot. Also, the whole area around it is mostly open grassland with only a couple trees here and there, so it's hard to approach without being seen.

Sure enough, after a few minutes I see a thin thread of smoke rising into the sky from about the middle of the biggest nest of rocks. I get my looking glass out and scan the nearby rocks. After a bit I catch sunlight on a gun barrel. Looking closely I can see a hat. Now I know where the sentry is posted. Unfortunately, I can't tell who it is.

The only thing for it is to wait until night. I don't want to waste the time—every minute I'm gone from Lily Creek has me worried that I guessed wrong, that Dace's men are running roughshod over it right now—but I won't be able to do Annie and the rest any good if I have a bullet in my head. It's only a few hours until sunset anyhow.

Once it's dark, I ride up to the nest of rocks real slow and easy, listening as I go. When I get close I can hear some voices echoing out of the rocks, but that's it. Sliding down off Coyote, I change into my moccasins, check my pistols and pull the Winchester out of its scabbard.

"Stay close, Coyote," I whisper to him, "In case I have to leave quick."

Coyote gives me a look. I know what it means. He's thinking if I'm too dumb to handle the likes of Boyce, then I deserve whatever happens to me.

"You're a hard case sometimes, you know that, Coyote?"

He wanders off and begins eating grass. Coyote may not hate me like he hates everyone else, but he's not exactly what you'd call an affectionate animal. Not even a nice one.

"Why do I put up with your sorry hide anyway?"

He swishes his tail and ignores me.

That's it. I got no more time to stand around and argue with a dumb animal, even one as smart as Coyote. I head on into the rocks.

It's easy to sneak up on them. They have a good-sized fire built and they're all sitting around it, staring into it. Even if one of them was to look straight at me he wouldn't be able to see anything, blinded by the light like that. You'd think, being outlaws, they'd know better.

I guess it's good they don't.

I see Slow Eye, Billy, Gimpy, Timmons and Wilson. That means we're just missing Boyce. I look around, making sure he's not sneaking up on me. I'm not letting him get the drop on me again.

The boys are arguing, as usual.

"I still say the queen of hearts is purtier than the other queens," Slow Eye says. He's got a card in his hands and is staring intently at it. Only he's holding it off to the side on account of he has one eye that doesn't point straight like it's supposed to.

"And I still say you're a damned idjit," Gimpy snaps. "All the queens look the same. Even a blind man knows that."

"No, there's something different about her. Something in her eyes."

"There's *nothing* in her eyes!" Gimpy shouts. "You been out here too long. You're seeing things."

"I bet that's why she's the one they talk about with lovers and all," Slow Eye muses, turning the card this way and that to better catch the firelight on it.

"I swear to god," Wilson says. "If you two don't shut up about this, I'm shooting you both. You been at this for an hour and I can't take any more of it."

"I'll shoot one of them too," Billy adds. "This ain't outlaw talk. We're supposed to talk about banks and trains and such."

"I think Slow Eye's right," Timmons ventures timidly.

"Nobody asked you," Gimpy barks. "Go back to whittlin' that...whatever that thing is supposed to be and shut up."

Timmons is whittling something. It looks like a piece of wood with a bunch of pieces shaved off. Nothing else.

"It's a woman," Timmons protests. "That woman we saw in Turkey Creek."

That brings groans from all the rest of them. "Don't start on about that woman again," Gimpy warns. "I can't listen to you pine about her no more."

"She smiled at me," Timmons says.

"No she didn't! She was grimacing. In fear. On account of you're so ugly." Gimpy pulls a face. "See this? It's a grimace. It's what people do when they're in pain or afraid. That's what she done."

"You're wrong," Timmons says. "We shared a moment. You cain't take that away from me."

Boyce comes clomping up then. "All you idiots shut the hell up right now."

"Still troubled by the runs are you, Boyce?" Gimpy chirps up.

"Ain't none of your damned business. But if I am it's your fault. I told you that meat had gone bad."

"No one else got sick," Gimpy says defensively.

"The hell you say," Wilson mutters. "I spent all last night with my britches around my ankles. I'm so sore I couldn't ride now if I had to."

I figure this is as good a time as any and I step out into the light.

"Howdy, gents."

40

Boyce jumps to his feet and starts to reach for his gun. Then he sees the Winchester pointing his way and he stops.

"What're you doing here?" he hisses.

I gesture with the barrel of the rifle. "I'm here to talk with the boys."

"Not happening. You want to talk to my gang, you talk to me."

"You fancy yourself a bad man, Boyce, but you're slow on the uptake."

He ponders this for a second. "You calling me dumb?"

"Yep. As a bag of rocks. But not the smart kind of rocks. The dumb ones. The real dumb ones."

His eyes narrow down and his lips pull back to show his teeth. "Them's fighting words."

"You think? See, there really is a brain trapped inside that lump of meat somewhere." I give him my own smile. "Here's a tip. I *meant* for those to be fighting words."

"You talk like a big man, you with a rifle and the drop on me."

"Oh, I'm happy to give you a fair shake, Boyce. I just want to make sure it's actually fair. You remember last time, don't you? Clubbing me over the head and all?"

"You shouldn't have turned your back on me."

"A mistake I will never make again."

"How you want to do this?"

"Anyway you like, Boyce. They're all going to end the same."

"Fists, then. Unless you're yellow without those shootin' irons."

"Good choice. Fists will be much more satisfying. Feeling your bones break will go a long way toward easing my troubled mind."

Boyce unbuckles his gun belt and tosses it aside. I hand my rifle to Billy. He's the only one I really trust.

"You'll see that this is clean, right?"

"You know it, Ace." Billy's excited, his Adam's apple bobbing up and down in his skinny throat. Sometimes I worry about Billy. He likes blood a little too much.

I take off my gun belt and turn back to Boyce. He's unbuttoning his shirt.

"Stack your duds and grease your skids," he says. "Cuz I'm going to tear down your meat house."

That stops me. "What in the world does *that* mean?"

"It means we're gonna fight."

"That's a damned peculiar way of putting it. I get the duds part," I say, taking off my duster and laying it across a log. I begin unbuttoning my shirt as well. "No sense in getting your blood on my duds. But 'grease your skids'?"

"It's from bare knuckle fighting," Wilson puts in. "The fighters grease their knuckles before a bout. Punches slide off. You don't tear the skin as much."

"Still a weird thing to say," I say.

"Enough with the talking," Billy says, his eyes dancing. "Tear down his meat house already."

"I should have shot you a long time ago," Boyce says to him.

"You coulda tried," Billy retorts. "Don't get saying confused with doing."

Boyce is bigger than me, with a longer reach and more heft. I need to keep him from closing with me. In a clinch he'll be able to use his size advantage. I need to stay at a distance, where I can use my speed. I'm glad I'm wearing my moccasins. They're a lot better for this.

Boyce charges me. He's not what you'd call a subtle man.

I duck under his first haymaker and give him a quick pair of jabs in the ribs. He grunts from the impact and I dance back before he can bring the other fist around.

A little murmur of approval comes from the watching men. They're gathered around us in a circle, eyes eager in the firelight.

"Did you like that?" I ask him. "I've got more."

"Love taps," he grunts. "My women punch harder than you."

"Maybe because your women are actually mules and they're sick of you pawing at them."

His face gets two shades darker and he really launches himself at me this time, trying to get me in a bear hug.

I slide to the side and tag him in the ear on the way by. That one hurt. I know because I've been hit there before.

"Hold still, mongrel!" he roars. "Stop running and face me like a man."

Now that riles me a little. Not the 'face me like a man' stuff, but the mongrel comment. I don't like slurs about my heritage.

"You want to dance?" I say. "Let's dance."

This time I charge him. I surprise him and get inside his defenses. I hit him in the gut with everything I have and as he starts to fold forward, I break his nose. He staggers back holding his nose, blood pouring out between his fingers.

He bends and pulls a knife out of his boot. Why am I not surprised?

"You're nothing but a bully, Boyce, you know that? You're big and tough until someone bloodies your nose and then all that yellow starts to show."

"I'll carve you up into Injun steaks," he howls, and comes at me, knife slashing wildly.

Big mistake. I'm Apache. Knife-fighting is our favorite sport. I've been playing this game since I could walk. Too many men get a knife in one hand and forget about everything else, thinking the knife will win the fight for them. I'm betting that Boyce is one of those.

He is.

He slashes down and across. I skip back so that the tip misses me, then slap his wrist down with my right hand. When I slap his wrist he stumbles forward, just a little, and his chin comes up. Like I expected, his left hand is waving around off to the side, not doing anything at all. He's wide open.

I give him a hard left square in the throat.

His eyes bug out and he grabs for his throat with his left hand. I take that opportunity to grab his other wrist. A twist and he drops the knife. Still holding his wrist, I bend it down and back behind him.

I kick him in the back of the legs and he goes down to his knees. Twisting his arm further up behind him, I force his face down into the dirt.

"Gonna get you," he rasps. At least that's what I think he says. His voice sounds all mashed up from the throat punch and it's hard to tell.

"You oughtta just kill him," Billy says. "He's only gonna cause trouble."

"Is he right, Boyce? Are you going to cause trouble?"

More garbled confusion. I can't make heads nor tails of this one, but it sure doesn't sound like an apology.

"Have it your way," I say. "You can thank me later for not killing you."

I give his arm a good jerk and there's an audible crack as it breaks. Boyce screams and passes out from the pain. I let him go and he flops in the dirt.

"Want me to kill him?" Billy asks.

I should let him. Boyce might repay me by shooting me in the back someday. But I can't do it. It's one thing to kill a man with a weapon in his hand, in a fair fight, but killing him when he can't fight back goes against the grain. It's a line I don't want to cross. I've known too many savages in my time, both white- and brown-skinned, and I don't want to be one of them.

"Leave him be, Billy."

I walk over and buckle on my gun belt, then retrieve the Winchester from Billy.

"That was over fast," Wilson says. He sounds disappointed. "I thought there'd be more blood."

I turn toward him. "Want to add some of yours?"

He takes a step back. "Not today."

Gimpy speaks up. "You broke his arm!" He says it like he just realized it. "What're we supposed to do now? He was the brains of this outfit."

"Which goes a long way toward explaining why nothing ever went right," Timmons says suddenly, surprising me. He comes over and pokes Boyce with the toe of his boot. He doesn't look too broken up about all this. Boyce always treated him poorly.

Correction. Boyce treated *everyone* poorly.

"Why'd you come here, anyway?" Slow Eye asks. "You fixin' to take over the gang?"

I start putting on my shirt. My knuckles are sore and a little scratched up. Maybe greasing them wouldn't be such a bad idea.

"I have a job for you boys."

"I knew it!" Billy says, rubbing his hands together. "I knew you had a job for us. What's it gonna be? A bank? Another train job?"

"Not like that at all. This is honest work for honest money."

The air goes out of all of them then, even Billy. "Well, shucks," Billy says. "You know I don't like working. It's how come I left the farm."

"It isn't that kind of work."

"I don't like any kind of work," Wilson says.

I finish with the shirt and put on my duster. "Okay, then. Guess I'll find someone else who wants to earn a thousand dollars."

"Now hold on!" Wilson yelps. The others look pretty alarmed too. "You didn't say nothing about a thousand dollars."

"A thousand dollars?" Slow Eye says, like he's never heard of a number that big before. "Between five people? Well, that'd be…that'd be…" He trails off, counting numbers in his head and ticking them off on his fingers. "A lot," he says finally. "More than I ever had."

"It's two hundred a piece. And there'll be no law chasing you after," I say.

The boys whoop and slap each other on the back. Except for Wilson. He's still staring at me suspicious-like.

"No normal job pays that much. What's the job?"

"Protecting a town."

"What?" Slow Eye says. "Like, from savage Injuns?" He realizes what he's said and holds his hands up. "No offense, Ace. They ain't all like you."

"And not all white folks are like you, Slow Eye. The stupidity is not being able to tell the difference."

Slow Eye's brow wrinkles while he tries to figure that one out.

Here comes the hard part. "You'll be protecting the town from Dace Jackson."

"Dace Jackson!" Gimpy yells. "Are you plumb loco?"

"Not going to do it," Timmons says.

"He'll kill us all," Wilsons says.

"I'm in, boss," Billy says. He looks like he's ready to go start killing right now. "We don't need these other dandies anyway. They're nothing but dead weight."

"Hey," Slow Eye says, "I ain't dead weight. I can shoot as good as any man." He's right there. I don't know why. You'd think with that misbehaving eye that he'd be an awful shot, but he's mostly dead on.

"If you're skeered, then just stay home," Billy sneers.

"I'm not scared," Gimpy protests. "I'm just not looking to get myself killed."

"Thanks," I tell Billy. "But I'll take it from here." I turn to the rest of them. "I could give you this big speech about how these are innocent people being threatened by a bad man, how there's widows and orphans and everything involved. I could even point out that it's a chance for you all to finally do something worthwhile with your miserable lives, how you could take this money and make an honest start for yourselves."

I pause, looking from one man to the other. The silence drags out.

"Well, are you gonna do that or not?" Gimpy finally says.

"No, I'm not. Instead I'm just going to tell you that you're doing this because this is my gang and you'll damned well do what I say." In a flash I have both pistols out, pointing at them. "Anyone have any arguments, you can take it up with the twins here."

Slow Eye puts his hands up. "You just tell me who to shoot, Ace."

"Better you than this shit heel telling us what to do," Timmons says. This time he gives Boyce a good kick in the ribs.

"Goddammit!" Gimpy yells. "I knew I shoulda just shot you from the rocks when I had a chance!" His shoulders slump. "I'm in."

Wilson gives me a poisonous look, but nods.

Billy whoops and throws his hat in the air. "Look out, Dace Jackson! Billy's boys are coming for you!"

"Don't call us that," Wilson snarls. "I ain't one of your boys."

"But we have to have a name," Billy protests. "Every gang has a name." He looks to me for support.

"Billy's boys?"

"I know, I know." He gets a hangdog look. "I just couldn't think of anything else and it sounds good."

"Keep working on it," I tell him. "Everyone saddle up. We're leaving right now."

41

We ride into town and I lead the boys over to the sheriff's office. Those that are talking shut up and everyone looks a mite uneasy. Not surprising, considering their histories.

Lou's out front, her hat down over her eye, her chair tilted back and a spittoon beside her. She pushes the hat up when we stop and her gaze moves over the gang, then comes to rest on me.

"Welcome back, Sheriff," she says. She reaches in her pocket, pulls out my star and flips it to me.

I have to admit. I enjoy the reactions of the gang. They're staring at me all bug-eyed, except for Billy, who looks a little pissed.

"You're the *sheriff*?" Slow Eye says. "Does that make us deputies?"

"You're the sheriff," Billy says flatly. "I reckon that's the end of all our talk of starting a gang together."

"That was you who did that talking, Billy. Not me." I swing down off Coyote.

"I want a star," Slow Eye says.

"If he gets one, I want one," Timmons says.

Gimpy crosses his arms. "I ain't working without a star."

"Okay, everyone gets stars."

"Not me," Billy says. "I'm an outlaw."

"No star for Billy, then. Wilson, how about you?"

"I want my two hundred dollars. I don't give a damn about no star."

"Quite the crew you have there," Lou says drily, and spits into the spittoon.

"When did you start using a spittoon?"

"Some of the ladies of the town brought it to me. They asked if I could please stop spitting on the streets of their home."

"I'm impressed. I didn't know you had it in you."

She shrugs. "They asked nice. And they brought cookies. But they're gone, so don't ask for any." She gestures at the gang.

162

Gimpy and Slow Eye are arguing about something. Timmons dropped his hat.

"You got a plan for them?"

"I have some ideas. For now I was thinking about taking them over to Pearl's and getting them fed."

"Are they gonna stay there too?"

"Where else would they stay?"

"They're gonna stink up my home."

"Listen to you, how fussy you've gotten. I'll tell them to take a dunk in the creek first, if that'll make you feel better."

"Them sleeping in the livery will make me feel better."

"Lou, we *need* them. Was there any trouble while I was gone?"

"Nary a sign."

From habit I look off to the west. No sign of anyone that way. "They're getting close. I can feel it."

"Are you ready?"

I roll my shoulders, trying to work out some of the knots there. "As much as I can be."

"I've been thinking about this. While you were gone."

"I thought you were spending all your time sleeping."

She gives me a look. "You want to hear what I have to say, or you want to crack wise?"

"I'm listening."

"There's only two of them, right? I say we put these new recruits of yours up on the roofs with rifles, shoot them the minute they wander into town. Assuming they *can* shoot, that is. Take the guess work out of the situation, so to speak."

I shake my head. "Can't do that."

"What? Why not?"

I tap the star, once again attached to my chest. "I'm the law. I have to do things lawful like."

"They tried to burn down the church. They've sworn to kill anyone who doesn't leave. They're coming to *kill* you! How dumb can you be?"

"Pretty dumb, I guess."

Lou fixes me with a red eye. "You're just like all the rest of them, ain't you?"

"I reckon I am."

"You don't care about those who care about you, the ones who will grieve when you're dead. All you care about is your foolish pride."

I turn away. There's nothing really I can say to her that will make any difference.

I get the gang situated and set Coyote up with a good bucket of oats. He's had a lot of work lately and he deserves it. Then I head on over to Annie's.

I'm up to the edge of her yard when there's movement in the trees and Virgil comes walking out, his squirrel gun over his shoulder.

"Didn't expect to see you there, you old coot. What gives?"

"Jist keeping an eye on Miss Annie. Knowing you're sweet on her, I had an idea them varmints might try going after her."

"I don't know what to say, Virgil." I really don't.

"Say I can shoot me a couple of them next time, instead of dumping water on them." He grins, showing off his tooth. "Even if it was fun, it ain't the same."

"There's going to be plenty of shooting before this is over. You have my word on that."

"That'll have to do, I guess. Well, go on in. Don't let me keep you out here. No doubt you'd rather look at her than me."

"No doubt."

I pause on Annie's front porch. There's a lot of emotions running through me. There's fear. What if she's changed her mind about me? There's hope. There's excitement.

I give up and knock on the door.

Annie opens it and my heart just falls clean down into my boots. I can't even breathe. She's like sunshine and cold water and my mother's best hug all rolled up into one.

"You're safe," she says, her face lighting up.

Before either of us can say more there are pounding feet and two little bodies hit my legs.

"Ace! Ace!" they yell. "You're back!"

I try to pat them on their heads but they're wriggling around like a couple of puppies and I keep missing. Finally I crouch down. "It's good to see you two."

"Mama's learning us our letters," little Diego says. "It's soooo boring!"

"Teaching," Annie corrects him. "Say teaching, not learning."

Meanwhile, Camila is talking a mile a minute, telling me all about a baby bird she found and how when she tried to put the nest back in the tree she fell and skinned her knee. It's hard to keep up, especially since Diego has started to growl and pretend to be a bear.

"Okay, children," Annie says. "That's enough. Let Ace breathe."

42

I'm in the sheriff's office with Lou. She's been like a cat in a roomful of rocking chairs all morning. She sits down for a minute, then gets up and goes to the window to look out. Then she paces. Goes back to sitting, back to the window, more pacing. She's making it powerful hard to stay calm.

"You think they'll come today?" she asks for the tenth time.

I don't even bother answering. I learned it doesn't matter what I say.

Finally, I've had enough. I put my hat on and stand up. "I'm going out to take a look around."

Lou, standing at the window, suddenly stiffens. She turns to me. "They're here."

I join her at the window. Riding up the street are two men.

It's them all right. The one on the right has a little tuft of mustache under his nose. By the mustache I know he's John Wesley Hardin. Hardin slouches in the saddle, a little fellow in gray clothes. To look at him, you wouldn't know he's one of the most feared men in the West. He looks like he'd jump at his own shadow. According to the stories, he once faced four men in a gunfight in Deadwood. Bullets were flying everywhere and he never so much as ducked or flinched, just kept shooting until they were all dead.

The other one is as clean-shaven as if he just came from the barber's. He looks to be wearing a new shirt and coat too. That's James Miller, or Killin' Jim as he's known by most. He's known for being fussy about his appearance. Word is he killed a man once for spilling soup on his shirt.

Looks like Dace is taking no chances.

They stop on the other side of the street, in front of the mercantile, and get off their horses, tie them to the hitching rail. They step out into the middle of the street and stand there, a half dozen paces apart.

And there they wait.

Lou grabs my arm suddenly and drags me around to face her. It always surprises me how strong she is. "Those are men who kill for a living. Men who'd think nothing of dry-gulching you."

"I know that."

"But it doesn't change anything, does it?"

I shake my head.

"We could shoot them from here. There's no chance a jury would convict you. Hell, they'd call you a hero."

I just stare at her. We've had this conversation and said all there was to say on it.

"You men are without a doubt the most frustrating, contrary creatures on God's green earth, you know that?"

"I know that too."

"You're going to get yourself killed!"

"Maybe. There's worse things than dying."

"Not to those you leave behind, the ones who'll grieve you."

I decide to try again, because I consider Lou my friend and what she thinks matters to me.

"I wasn't completely honest with you yesterday, Lou. It's not just the star. It's me. It's what it will do to me."

"You're not making any sense." She bites off each word like it angers her.

"If I gun them down like that I'll change. I'll cross a line that I can never go back over."

I don't think it's working. She's still looking at me plenty angry.

"You coming out, Sheriff?" one of the men calls. "Or do we have to come in after you?"

"I'm coming out!" I yell back. I look at Lou again.

"Do you know what *Netdahe* means? It's an oath some Apache warriors take, an oath to be always at war, to fight and kill the enemy as long as he still lives." I tap my chest. "The desire to live the *Netdahe* life is in here. I can feel it there always. It doesn't always seem like such a bad thing, you understand? A lot of times I *want* to take it.

"Things get a lot simpler once you take the *Netdahe* oath. You don't have to make decisions, they're all already made for you."

I think about Geronimo then, the darkness that hovers around him, engulfed as he is in *Netdahe*. The same darkness that's around the braves who follow him. I realize then why I never liked him. It's because I've always been afraid of how easily I could be just like him.

I realize also that part of the reason I left my clan and went out to live amongst the white man was because I wanted to see if there was another way, if I could learn to see the white man— and the half of me that is white—as something other than my enemy.

"I don't want to live my life at war."

"You're afraid if you go past that line, you'll never come back," Lou says in a soft voice.

"I'll kill and kill and it won't ever be enough."

Lou's looking at me differently now. The angry lines in her face have smoothed and there's other lines there now. Lines of sadness.

"Okay," she says. "I still don't understand it, but I accept it." I turn to go and she grabs my arm. "Can you do this? Can you take them both?"

"I don't know. I guess we'll find out."

43

One last check on my guns, then I drop them back in my holsters. Settle my hat firmly on my head and push open the door.

It opens with a squeak of protesting hinges. I step through and onto the little porch. It feels good there in the shade. It's noon and the sun is very bright, hotter than normal too. For a brief moment I stand there and savor it.

Life is a lot sweeter when it's about to end.

I'm surprised at how calm I feel. I look at the sky, the mountain peaks in the distance, the clouds hanging around them. If these are my last moments in this life, I feel at peace.

Last I look at the two gunfighters. They're staring at me, faces expressionless. Both are wearing their shooting irons tied down low. Killin' John's is on his left, something I plant in my mind for later. They're holding perfectly still. Maybe they're statues, like the ones I saw at the General's place.

"You men are under arrest," I say. "I trust you'll come peacefully. Our jail cell's small, but seeing's how close you two are already, I don't think you'll mind it."

"Don't talk foolishness," John Hardin says. He's sure not a very big man. But then, that gun on his hip means he doesn't have to be. "You know it won't be like that."

"How will it be then? Tell me."

"We'll make it quick," Killin' Jim says. "A few seconds and it will all be over. We'll ride on. You'll lie in the dirt."

I shake my head. "I don't like that ending to the story. How about you listen to a new one?"

"Why not?" Killin' Jim says. "It won't change anything."

"How about I shoot you both dead and neither of you rides on? The good folks of this town live happy ever after. That's a better story for everyone, don't you think?"

"Not for us," Hardin says.

"No, not for you, I suppose." I scratch my jaw. "I guess there's no way this works out happy for everyone, is there?"

"Let's get this over with," Killin' Jim says. He sounds bored. This is just another job to him and I'm nothing but a tin pot sheriff he needs to take care of, a bug to be stomped on before he can collect his money.

I walk out into the street, circling around until I'm standing in the middle of the street, about fifty paces away. They turn as I do, always facing me, eyes wary.

"I've never really done this, you know," I call out to them. "Am I doing this right?"

"It'll do," Killin' Jim says.

"How do we know when to start? Are we supposed to count or something?"

"You'll know. You can even start if you like."

"Well, that's neighborly of you. Or it would be, if you weren't here to kill me. Sure you gents won't change your mind? Pearl made the sweetest cherry pie this morning. I could probably wrangle you each a piece."

I'm watching them real close while I talk and it feels like I can almost see it start to happen even before Hardin himself knows it's going to. I don't know what gives it away, a tightening of the muscles in his right arm, a tilt to the head, but all at once I know it's coming.

John Hardin grabs for his gun. At practically the same instant Killin' Jim goes for his, like they were in secret communication or something.

It's almost a surprise to me to feel the Colts in my hands, it happens so clean and smooth. I don't remember making the decision or doing it, they're just there. Time slows down, everything happening clear and etched on my mind.

The left gun goes off slightly before the right. Flame stabs from the end of the muzzle and the slug smashes into Hardin's hip just a fraction before he fires. His bullet whines by my ear as he's turned halfway around.

A sudden widening of Killin' Jim's eyes as he realizes I beat him. Probably never been beat before. First time for everything, right?

My right-hand Colt bucks in my hand and a .45-caliber piece of lead catches him low in the stomach. He staggers back, his gun still coming up.

It barks and I feel a sudden hot burst of pain on the side of my neck.

The left goes off again, and a bright spot of blood appears high on Hardin's chest just as he's turning back to shoot at me again. For some reason he doesn't go down straight away and his lips pull back in a snarl as he jerks his trigger.

The bullet hits me on the outside of the knee and my leg buckles enough that my next shot—the one meant to take Killin' Jim in the head—only grazes his face.

Time returns to normal and the day becomes a chaos of screaming lead, tongues of flame, blood and smoke, all of us firing as fast as we can.

My hammers fall on empty. Through the drifting clouds of smoke I see that Killin' Jim is down, flat on his back, arms flung wide like he's offering an embrace to the sky.

John Hardin is on his knees, his gun held out pointing at me, the hammer clicking on empty cylinders over and over. He's bleeding pretty much everywhere. It looks like none of my shots missed him.

I walk toward him, limping from my wounded knee. It still works, so that's something. There's a lot of blood running down the side of my neck but I'm not bled out yet so the bullet didn't hit an artery. A good day, all in all.

I stop in front of Hardin. His lips work as he tries to say something.

"You're dead, Hardin. You just haven't accepted it yet."

He frowns, a line appearing between his eyes.

"Who...who are you?" he finally manages to whisper.

"I'm the sheriff of Lily Creek, that's who I am. And you're nobody."

He ponders this for a moment, then topples over dead.

44

"Whoo-eee!" Billy shouts, busting out the door of the mercantile and running into the street. "That was some damned fine shootin', Ace! I never seen the like!" Behind him comes Slow Eye and Timmons. Gimpy limps along in the rear.

I drop the Colts back into their holsters. Suddenly I'm feeling awfully tired.

All up and down the street people are coming out of shops and homes and heading my way. I wish they'd stay away. I want to be alone right now.

"You got 'em both, Ace, John Wesley Hardin and Killin' Jim," Billy crows, slapping me on the shoulder. He's practically dancing, he's so excited. "I didn't know there was a man alive could do that."

"Don't touch him," Lou snaps. "Can't you see the man's injured?"

"But they're only scratches," Billy protests.

"Come on, Ace," Lou says, her voice surprisingly gentle. "Let's get you inside and look at those wounds."

"Bring him down to my house," Annie says. Where'd she come from? "I have some bandages already laid out and water on to boil."

"There's no need to fuss," I say. "It's like Billy said. They're only scratches."

"And that's why your boot is filling up with blood," Lou says sarcastically.

I look down. There does seem to be quite a lot of blood.

"We're not arguing about this," Annie says. "Get in."

I hear a noise and look up to see Ancil pull up in a little one-horse buggy. "It's not far. I can walk."

"Get in, you damned fool," Lou snaps. "Or I'll throw you in."

"All right. There's no need to push. I'm getting." Hands help me climb up onto the seat next to Ancil and that's not a bad thing either. The initial rush of the gunfight is wearing off and I'm starting to hurt. My leg doesn't seem to want to bend anymore.

I settle onto the seat and look around. It looks like the whole town has turned out, all of them staring up at me openmouthed. For some reason my eyes fall on Herm. He's standing in the back, glaring at me. I wave at him and call out. "Better luck next time!" He turns on his heel and stomps off.

"That man is a snake," I tell Ancil.

"I'm not one to speak ill of others," Ancil says, snapping the reins to start the horse moving, "but in this case I'm inclined to agree."

"You know he's working for Jackson, don't you? Dace is paying Herm off to convince you folks to leave town."

Ancil sighs. "It's not the most surprising news I've heard. Some of us have discussed the possibility."

"What do you aim to do about it?"

"We don't. We're just going to keep an eye on him."

"You all are a lot more patient than I am."

"How's the knee?"

Wincing, I flex it. "It'll heal."

"Annie knows what she's doing. She'll fix you up."

"They're only going to keep coming, Ancil. Sooner or later I won't be fast enough." Ever since I noticed that the Hashknife is holding roundup there's been an idea working around in the back of my mind. It's growing a few new shoots now.

"I think it's time we take the fight to them," I say.

Ancil gives me a speculative look but says nothing.

He helps me inside Annie's house. I start to sit down at the dining table but Annie cuts in.

"In there." She points to her bedroom. "Lie down on the bed."

"I can't do that," I protest. "I'll get blood on your blankets."

"Then I'll wash them."

I don't seem to have a lot of choice. Ancil still has a hold of my arm and he's steering me that way firmly. There's a lot of steel in those muscles. I probably couldn't get away if I tried.

"Get him undressed," she tells Ancil. "I'll go get the bandages and water."

Once again my protests don't seem to matter much. Before I can say a word I'm flat on my back on the bed and Ancil is tugging on my boots. "Are you going to pull your pants off yourself, or make me do it?" he asks. "The shirt comes off too."

I feel panicky, a whole lot more afraid than I was during the gunfight. "You can't expect me to be naked in her bed, Ancil. Can't we just roll my pant leg up or something?"

"Don't be a baby," he says, a little crossly it sounds like. "We don't have a doctor here and Annie is the best we have at dressing wounds. You won't be the first man she's tended to, and you won't be the last. If you're that scared you can wrap the blanket around you, leave only your leg sticking out. But the pants are coming off."

I quit fighting. It's clear this fight I can't win. But when Annie comes back in the room, I'm ready for her. I've got the blanket wrapped around every bit of me I can, only my lower left leg and my head sticking out.

"I think your patient will cooperate now," Ancil says. "I'll send Pearl along to make sure. I'm going to go help bury those men."

Annie kneels down on the floor and sets down the water and the bandages. She checks my neck wound first. "Looks like it's mostly stopped bleeding. Hold this against it." She gives me a bandage and I press it to my neck.

She starts cleaning my knee up. "You got lucky," she says. "The bullet tore out a chunk of flesh, but it looks like it missed the bone. If it eases your mind any, I was in training at a local hospital when my father decided to move us out west. I've done more than my share of bandaging and stitching."

A few minutes later she has the knee wrapped up tight and a couple minutes after that my neck wound is too.

"There," she says, her voice all calm and professional. "You'll be good as new in a few days."

"Thank you."

Kneeling down beside me, she puts her fingers on my cheek. Her touch is light and soft. "Thank you, Ace. For…everything."

Then the most remarkable thing happens. She starts shaking and tears begin running down her face.

"What's wrong?" I ask, suddenly alarmed.

"I just...I just..." Suddenly she grabs my hands fiercely and presses her cheek against mine, her whole body shaking with sobs. "I was so afraid. I thought those men were going to kill you."

"No, there was never any—"

She pulls back and glares at me. "Don't you say that, Ace. Don't you dare! Don't act like nothing could happen to you. I've seen too much. I know how quickly the world takes away and I won't have you acting like that."

I'm stunned. I'm not sure what to say or do.

"I've been in tight spots before..."

"And you got lucky. But maybe next time you won't be. Promise me, Ace, promise me you'll fight and stay vigilant. Stay alive. I can't lose any more people that I...that I care about."

"I promise."

"That's better." She wipes at her tears and tries to smile.

The door opens and Pearl comes in. She looks at both of us and wisely decides to say nothing except "I don't believe I'm needed here, am I?"

She backs out and closes the door behind her.

45

"It's time to take the fight to them," I say.

I've gathered the gang, Lou and Virgil together. It's been a couple days since the gunfight and my wounds are healing up nicely, though my knee is stiff and still pretty painful.

"Now you're talking," Billy says, taking out his pistol and waving it around. "Let's shoot some of those sonsabitches."

"I like the way this young feller thinks!" Virgil cackles, rubbing his gnarly old hands together. "We'll hit 'em like the wrath of God."

"What do you have in mind?" Lou says. She looks wary. "I won't go along with anything foolhardy."

"Don't go passing judgment until you hear his plan," Billy protests. "Ace knows what he's doing." He looks worried suddenly. "You *do* know what you're doing, don't you? I don't want to seem picky, but that whole idea about dropping the safe off the cliff...that didn't work too good."

That makes me wince. Saying it didn't work too well isn't saying the half of it. "No safes this time, Billy. I guarantee it." Safes and I don't get along all that well.

"Why don't we talk about the plan I come up with?" Gimpy cuts in.

"Because it's a stupid plan," Billy retorts. "Building a wall around the whole town. You know how long that'd take?"

"I'm not building any walls," Wilson says darkly. "I signed on to shoot, not work."

"You never even gave my plan a chance," Gimpy squawks. "If we just get a bunch of men on axes and go to work felling trees—"

The others shout him down before he can get any further. When he still won't shut up Virgil takes off his coonskin hat and slaps him across the face with it.

"Hey! What'd you go and do that for?" Gimpy cries. Then, "God almighty, that thing stinks! Get it out of my face!"

"Everyone just shut up for a minute," I say. "Hear me out."

It takes a minute for them to settle down and while they do I swap a look with Lou, who's clearly disgusted.

"This was the best you could do?" she asks me in a low voice.

"I'm starting to see why Boyce was always threatening to shoot someone," I reply.

Finally, they're quiet. "It's roundup over at the Hashknife. Has been for the last week or two. From the looks of it, they're gathering everything. Probably planning on driving a few thousand steers down to the railhead and shipping them off."

"So now we're cattle rustlers?" Wilson says. "Is that it?"

I give him a hard look until he backs down, muttering to himself.

I point at the sky. Some big thunderheads are building off to the west. "It's been threatening to rain every day lately, lots of thunder and lightning. Thunder and lightning makes cows nervous."

Lou's the first one to see where I'm going with this. "That's crazy. It's a crazy idea. But if it works..." She lets off a low whistle.

"What're you all talking about?" Slow Eye asks. "What idea? I didn't hear no idea."

Billy catches on next. "You're a goddamned genius, Ace."

"Now I'm getting angry," Gimpy says. "I still don't know what you're taking about."

"I'm talking about a stampede," I say. "Ten thousand frightened longhorns running wild, destroying everything in their path."

46

We ride out after dark, eight of us all told. The wind is blowing pretty good by then and the night sky is lost behind massive banks of clouds. Lightning flickers and thunder rumbles. It's perfect. The herd should be good and nervous.

"Now remember what I said." I have to raise my voice a little to be heard over the coming storm. "Don't shoot anyone if you don't have to. We're trying to convince the regular hands, the cowboys, to leave. There's no need to kill them."

"What if they need killing?" Virgil asks.

I knew he'd say that. The old coot is downright dangerous. How he lived to get this old is beyond me.

I decide to try and explain it to him, to all of them, one more time. "Most of the hands on the Hashknife are just regular cowboys, signed up to do a job. If we make it hot enough for them, get them to see that it's not healthy to stick around, I'm betting that most will drag their freight and pull out."

"Being dead ain't healthy," Virgil mutters.

I ignore him and continue on. "Once they leave, we can deal with what's left. There can't be that many who are ready to kill for hire. Once we know who they are, we can make a plan to deal with them."

"Could be those who are left will be so busy cleaning up the mess that they won't have time to come after Lily Creek. Buy us some breathing room," Timmons says.

That surprises me. I didn't know that boy had all that much going on upstairs. "Timmons is right. Could be some of the fight will go out of them. Dace Jackson might even decide Lily Creek is too much trouble and back off altogether."

I don't really believe that, but hey, I can hope. You never know how much sand a man's got in him until you punch him in the nose good and hard. I've seen big, tough-looking men decide they don't really want to fight once they see some of their own blood.

"I hope they don't give up too easy," Billy says, drawing his gun yet again. He's already drawn it about ten times since we started out. Maybe he and Virgil are long-lost kin.

The storm keeps building as we ride on through the night. By the time we get close there's lightning flickering nearly constantly and the thunder sounds like war drums in the sky. I pull up and motion the others to stop. Ahead we can see the dark mass of the herd.

Like I expected, they're on their feet, milling around, mooing. They're on edge, the fear of each one infecting the ones around them. A cow herd might look like a mass of individuals, but when it gets scared it's really a single creature with thousands of parts. Right now that creature has no focus, no direction. But with the right push it will have direction and it will roar across this valley like a flash flood.

In the periodic flashes of lighting I can see cowboys moving along the edge of the herd, calling out to the cattle, singing to them, trying to keep them calm. There's enough of them that it's working so far, but they're a pretty fragile dam holding back a lot of pent-up fear. They won't count for much once the stampede starts.

I've brought us around so we come up on the side of the herd away from the ranch headquarters. My hope is that we'll be able to get the stampede to thunder right on through there. They'll do a lot of damage on the way, maybe enough to cripple Dace's whole operation.

"Spread out!" I call to the others, raising my voice to be heard over the wind and the thunder. "When you hear my shots, give it everything you got!"

The rest disappear off into the gloom. I give them a few minutes until I judge they're in position, then I lean over Coyote's neck.

"It's time to run, boy!" I yell and tap him in the ribs with my heels. I don't wear spurs. Never do. I don't have to do much to encourage him. Coyote likes to run.

We race through the grass toward the herd. As we get close a nearby cowboy turns and looks in our direction. There's a flash of lightning and his expression—mouth open, shouting something I can't hear—is oddly clear for a moment.

I start shooting and hollering. Within seconds gunfire erupts on both sides of us as the others join in.

At first nothing happens. The nearest cattle stare at us in confusion.

Then a lightning bolt stabs to the earth nearby, close enough that I can feel the concussion. The crack of thunder is huge and nearly simultaneous.

The stampede begins.

Bellowing madly, the herd turns and begins charging off in the other direction. There's nothing the cowboys can do, nothing anyone can do. The cowboys take off running, trying to get around the herd, trying to find the leaders and head them off, but it will be hours and miles before they manage that.

Coyote and I gallop along after. There's no need to. There's nothing left for us to do. The boulder is rolling downhill. All we need to do is stay out of the way.

But I want to see. I want to know the destruction firsthand.

I'm not the only one either. One by one the others materialize around me. The rain starts to fall, coming down in blinding waves. The world is bolts of fire, crashing doom and sheets of water.

It's almost like we're stampeding too. We run after the herd in wild, reckless abandon, firing our guns and screaming like madmen.

We come to the headquarters after a few minutes. About that time the rain starts to slacken. We all stop and stare openmouthed at the havoc we have wrought.

All the corrals are gone, swept away and stomped into toothpicks by the herd. The smaller buildings are gone as well, only bits of foundation remaining. One whole corner of the blacksmith's shop has been torn away and a section of the roof has collapsed. There's a flicker of flames inside and it looks like it's spreading. A side porch has been torn off the main house and a piece of wall is stove in.

"Wow," Timmons says.

"I never seen the like," Slow Eye adds.

"It's beautiful," Billy says.

"It looks like an avalanche went through here," Lou says.

"You think they'll know we've been here?" Gimpy asks, giving a low chuckle.

"Let's make sure of it," I say. I lead them over to the bunkhouse. The place looks like it held up pretty well, only a corner of it ripped away. Some cowboys are emerging from it, looking around them in disbelief.

I ride up to them. "You boys know what just happened here, don't you?"

"Biggest damn stampede I ever saw," one of them says.

"True. But that's not really what happened." They look up at me, confused. "What happened is you fellers just became unemployed. Understand? You got no jobs."

"What're you talking about? Who are you?"

"I'm the sheriff of Lily Creek, that's who I am. And these are my deputies." From the corner of my eye I see Slow Eye pointing at the star on his chest. Even since Ancil made it for him he can't stop bragging on it. It's not much more than a piece of tin quickly cut in the shape of a star, but the way he wears it you'd think it was made of gold.

"Your boss has been fixing to run us off. This is to show you that we won't be run off. Not by you, not by anybody."

The cowboys look at us, at the guns in our hands, and there's a general movement backwards. "Listen, Sheriff," one of them says. "We don't want no trouble. We're just hired hands."

"Then you'll get no trouble," I tell them. "Pack your poke and ride on out. I'll give you one day. After that any man left on this spread is to be considered an outlaw and my deputies are authorized to shoot you on sight."

"I want no part of this," one of them says.

"Me either," says another. "You won't see me around." Mutters of agreement from the rest.

"Spread the word," I tell them. "The same applies to every man here."

Then I wheel Coyote around and we head back to town.

47

Word spreads fast about what we did and soon the whole town is buzzing about the stampede. People are all smiley and everyone wants to shake our hands. The gang is strutting around town like they just lassoed the moon and squeezed butter out of it. Well, everyone but Wilson. He's still scowling like he sat on a bumblebee.

"I don't like it," I tell Lou. We're in the sheriff's office and it's two days since the stampede. This time she's sitting and I'm pacing.

"Kinda nice, being a hero," she says. "A body could get used to it."

"They're acting like we already won and we haven't."

Lou looks up at me with a question in her one eye.

"All we've done is kicked over the hornet's nest."

"You saying now that it wasn't a good idea?" I can tell she thinks I'm crazy. "Maybe you're tired. You ain't been getting much sleep."

"It's not that." I am tired though. I was out all last night scouting, making sure no one was sneaking up on us. "I just feel it's way too soon to start celebrating."

"They been under a lot of strain, the folk of this town. Maybe they just need to celebrate a little. Let 'em have their fun."

I go to the window and look out, then groan. Wilson's coming. The man is wet socks on an icy day. He carries his own cloud around with him.

He's barely in the door before he says, "When am I getting my money?"

Lou gives me a look. Clearly she's wondering what money I promised him and where I'm planning on getting it.

"You'll get it when the job's done."

"I saw what we did to their headquarters. It's two days and no one has showed up. I call that done." His eyes narrow down. "Unless you don't have the money. That's not it, right?"

"Of course I have the money," I reply, hoping like crazy that Annie really does have it. I can't help but remember Herm's words about it. "But you're not getting paid until the job is done."

"It *is* done."

"Saying it's done doesn't make it so," Lou says.

"Who asked you?" Wilson snaps.

Lou doesn't answer, just spits and wipes her chin.

It takes a couple minutes, but I get Wilson out of the office. I see Billy down the street and get an idea.

"Hey, Billy."

"What's up, chief?"

"I need you to do something."

"Whatever you say."

"Ride on over to the Hashknife. Act like you're a hand looking for work. Suss out what's going on and come back and tell me."

"That's a good idea," he says. "I could be like a spy." He starts to walk away, then turns back. "What name should I give them?"

I give him a blank look. "It doesn't matter what name you give them. They don't know you from Adam."

"Darn it, Ace. Spies ain't supposed to use their real names. I have to have a fake one."

I say the first name that comes to mind. "Henry."

He shakes his head. "I hate that name. My dad's name is Henry."

"Then pick another one!"

His eyes widen. "You're a little touchy today, boss. You know that?"

"I just don't see what difference the name makes."

"Spies get caught over little things like that."

"Just go, Billy. It'll take you a couple hours to get there. You can think up a name on the way."

"I need a back story too."

My headache's feeling worse. I want to choke him. "Make that up while you're at it."

"I'll tell them I'm the son of a rich plantation owner, what lost everything in the war."

"You don't have a Southern accent."

"Y'all don't know what yore talking about," he says, in what must be the worst Southern accent ever.

"Don't do an accent, Billy. Just be yourself. Learn what you can. Wait till dark and come back."

"You can count on me, Ace." He salutes and hustles off to get his horse.

I turn and see Lou is watching from the porch. "They're not the brightest bunch, that old gang of yours."

"Someday I'll tell you about the time we tried to rob a train. You probably don't know this, but a safe will bounce."

"Can't say I did know that. Doesn't seem like what you'd call useful information."

"It would've been useful to us."

48

I go out scouting after dark again. The hours pass and there's no sign of Billy. I hope they didn't catch him. Finally, I head back into town, thinking maybe he slipped by me somehow.

It's around midnight and there's a light in the sheriff's office. I go in and find Lou in there. She looks up when I come in.

"Coffee on the stove," she says.

I pour myself a cup. "Any sign of Billy?"

Lou shakes her head.

"I think I'm going to head on over there and have a look."

"That's a bad idea, Ace. They know you."

Footsteps on the porch and we both turn. It's Billy. "I'm back!" he says, like we couldn't tell by looking at him.

"What did you learn?"

"The hands are all gone, every single one of them. The place is a ghost town. The ones that're left damn sure ain't cowboys. A saltier lot you never saw. I recognized a couple of them."

"How many are there?"

"About twenty."

That's bad. "Did you hear anything about what they're planning?"

"Not really. Just some stuff about finishing this off once and for all. No more half-measures. It sounds to me, Ace, like next time they're coming in force to clean us out."

"Any idea when?"

He shakes his head. "It's gonna be a couple days, though. They said they're waiting for a few more men to join them."

Strangely, knowing they're coming makes me feel calmer. Ideas about how to defend the town start rattling around in my head.

There's shouting from out back suddenly. Lou snatches up the lantern and we hustle out of the sheriff's office and head around back. There we find Virgil holding Herm at the end of his rifle.

"Lookit me!" he crows. "I caught a skunk!"

"Sheriff, I demand you arrest this man," Herm cries. "He has assaulted me." He has a cut on his cheek.

"Shut yer mouth or I'll cut you again," Virgil barks. He looks at me. "I caught this man robbing the bank."

"Nonsense," Herm stammers. "I'm the banker. Why would I rob my own bank?"

"Drop it, Herm," I tell him. "We both know why."

"He threw something off into the bushes yonder," Virgil says, pointing.

Billy goes off and returns pretty quickly with a carpet bag. He opens it and looks inside. "It's full of money, all right."

Herm wilts. "You still can't prove anything. I have a right to a fair trial."

"Hold on," Lou says. "I have a better idea, something more fitting for a rat like this." The smile she gives Herm is downright evil and he goes white and starts shaking.

"You can't hang me without a trial," he protests. "That's nothing but a lynching and you'll be murderers."

"I wasn't talking about hanging you."

"What is it?" Billy asks. He's getting that too-excited look in his eyes again. "Does it involve knives?" There's no doubt the kid is touched in the head.

"I saw the cooper was making some new barrels this afternoon and earlier in the day a couple of the ladies were butchering chickens," Lou says.

Billy frowns. "I don't get it. We gonna put him in a barrel with some chickens? What good will that do?"

"No good at all. But that ain't what I'm thinking of doing. Billy, go get as many of those chicken feathers as you can. I'm going to pay a visit to the cooper's. Virgil, haul this varmint around to the street and wait for me there." When Billy hesitates, she says, "You're going to like this, Billy. Trust me."

They head out and Herm turns to me. "Sheriff, I demand to be taken into custody."

"I think you lost the option to demand anything when you tried to rob the good people of this town, Herm."

He grabs onto my coat with shaking hands. "You have to protect me! It's your job!"

186

"Sure. I'll protect you." I remove his hands. "I'll make sure Billy doesn't get carried away and kill you."

Virgil wheezes with laughter. "Notice how he didn't say nothing about me?"

Herm backs away, his eyes wide.

"That includes you, Virgil. You're not doing any killing either."

He gives me a black look. "Lotsa times I don't think much of you, Sheriff."

"I'll try not to let it keep me up nights, Virgil."

We head around front. A few minutes later Billy shows up with a sack of chicken feathers. But it's not until I see Lou pushing a wheelbarrow up the street with a tub of some black stuff in it that I realize what she's up to.

Lou stops and dips her finger in the tub. It comes out smeared in tar. "We got lucky. The coals weren't all the way dead yet so it's still warm."

Herm doesn't look like he feels too lucky. "You can't do this to me," he quavers.

"Hell," Billy says, "the way I see it, you done this to yourself."

"Nothing like a good, old-fashioned tar-and-feathering to teach a rascal a lesson," Lou cackles. She sounds positively evil. "Billy, Virgil, would you be so good as to strip him down?"

Billy and Virgil don't need to be asked twice. Herm tries to fight, but he's all soft and paunchy. Apparently the banking business doesn't build a lot of muscle. They knock him down pretty easy and start tugging on his coat.

"Stop squirmin'!" Virgil says. "It ain't gonna change nothing."

Finally, the coat comes off. When they try to take his shirt off it just rips and they toss the pieces aside.

The shoes are easy. Billy sits on Herm's chest while Virgil wrestles his leg like it's a calf that needs branding. But when they go for his pants, Herm starts making this squealing noise. It's high-pitched and not pleasant on the ears.

"Just cut them off," Billy says. "I can't stand listening to him holler."

Virgil's knife comes out and Herm's squealing gets louder, but it's like Virgil said, it doesn't change anything.

I realize I should probably stop them. I don't know much about the sheriff business, but this probably isn't what you'd call exactly lawful. But the way I see it, Herm sold out his own neighbors to the enemy and then he tried to make off with all their money. In a lot of towns that would earn him a long drop at the end of a short rope, so maybe he should count himself lucky.

Pants off, Billy gets off Herm's chest and grabs his arms. Virgil gets his legs and they stretch him out. Herm has quit fighting now and is just lying there moaning. There's a big brush sticking out of the tar and Lou takes it out and slaps it down on his stomach.

That gets him started again. Herm squalls and thrashes around. "It burns!" he yells.

"If it wasn't hot, it wouldn't spread," Lou says, dunking the brush back in the tub. "Then we'd have to find some other way to teach you a lesson and it might not be so pleasant. 'Sides, it ain't that hot."

When she's painted his front side I grab up the sack of feathers Billy fetched and shake half over him. The feathers float down and stick to him like a second skin.

Gimpy, Slow Eye and Timmons come running up.

"You're having a tar and feather party and you didn't invite me?" Gimpy yells.

"Maybe you all shouldn't waste so much time sleeping," Billy retorts.

"All you had to do was give a holler," Slow Eye says.

"Reckon Herm here did that for us," Billy replies. "The front looks good, Virgil. Let's flip him over."

While they're doing that, Lou holds out the brush. Gimpy, Slow Eye and Timmons fight over it for a bit and Timmons ends up with a blotch of tar in his hair, but in the end each of them gets to plaster on some and then I dump the rest of the feathers on him.

Billy and Virgil let go of him and stand up.

At first Herm lies there, whimpering. "Get up," Gimpy says. "Do something." The boys are having fun and they don't want it to end.

Slowly, Herm hauls himself to his feet. He looks a sight, feathers sticking out everywhere. "What do I do now?" he moans.

"Start walking," Lou says.

"Where do I go?"

"Why, to the Hashknife, of course. They own you, don't they?" The woman is ruthless.

"Wilkins hates me."

"You ain't too popular around here neither," Billy says.

"It's too far."

"No it's not. It's not more than fifteen miles. You'll be there before you know it," Lou says. I'm thinking that I want to remember not to cross this woman.

"At least let me take a horse."

"If you don't like walking, I'd be happy to get my horse and drag you," Billy says.

That decides him. Herm sets off down the street.

"Is that it?" Timmons says, sounding kind of sad.

"For now, Timmons," I tell him. "For now."

49

I walk into the Pearl's dining room the next morning and slump down in my chair, rubbing my eyes. Lou and the gang are already there, spread out across the room. Lou hands me a cup of coffee.

"From how you look, I take it you haven't come up with a plan yet," she says.

"No. I was awake most of the night thinking about it."

"I still say we build a wall," Gimpy says. "Like the army forts. All we need is to start cutting down trees."

"Shut up about the wall already," Wilson says. "You know how many trees that would take, how much work that'd be?"

"We don't have the time for something like that anyway," I say. "According to what Billy says, they're going to be coming in the next couple days."

"Why don't we put everyone up on the roofs? Hide until they get into the middle of town, then we shoot them down," Billy says.

"Because that's what they'll be expecting," Lou says.

"We'd get a lot of them that way, but I think we'd all get ourselves killed too," I say.

Slow Eye looks alarmed. "I ain't in favor of any plan what gets me killed. I can't spend that money if I'm dead."

"What we need is a trap," Timmons says. "Something we can lure them into, get 'em caught up so's they don't have the time to be shooting at us. Like how you trap a bear or a cougar. It can't get at you with its paw caught."

"And everyone said my idea was dumb," Gimpy snorts. "Bear traps for men. I never heard anything dumber."

"Hold on a second," I say. Timmons' words have triggered an idea. "You may have something there. Any of you men handy with an axe?" I ask.

"Why? You're not thinking about going along with Gimpy's fool idea, are you?" Wilson says.

"I cleared forty acres of woodland for my pa back in Tennessee before I was ten," Timmons says. "I can make the chips fly."

"Not me," Billy says. "Me and axes don't get along."

"I can drop a tree faster than any man here," Gimpy says.

"No, you can't," Timmons says.

"Bet me," Gimpy says. "I'll show you. I bet I can drop two trees before you drop one."

"With those skinny little arms you got?" Timmons says. "You probably can't even lift an ax."

I cut in before the arguing gets out of hand. "Settle it later. We don't have the time right now. You two go around town and find a couple axes. Sharpen them up and meet me at the far end of town, where that little path leads on down through the trees to the creek."

I turn to Lou and Slow Eye. "Go down to the livery stable. We need the heaviest rope you can find, at least four hundred feet of it. Once you get it, start splicing it together and meet me in the same place."

Billy says, "What can I do?"

"I need you to keep watch. Get out to that little pass a couple miles outside town and keep an eye out. Once you see them coming, get back here quick and let us know." I notice that Wilson doesn't ask what he can do. That man does nothing at all unless he has to.

I head on down to Annie's. She's standing out by the street talking to Pearl.

"I need you two to go around to everybody in town. Tell them to be ready to clear out on a moment's notice."

"We're not running are we?" Pearl asks.

"No. We're setting a trap. But for it to work I need to make them think we have. Pick a spot way back in the forest, at least a mile from town. Tell everyone when they hear the church bell ring they're to head for that spot and keep their heads down."

Pearl bustles off. Annie pauses for a moment and looks at me. "I believe in you," she says. "I know you can defeat them."

I sure hope so. It's kind of a crazy plan. But aloud I say, "It'll work. They won't know what hit them."

She gives me a quick hug and I head off to do some looking around.

The path at the far end of town leads into a good-sized patch of pine trees, some of them pretty tall. After about a fifty yards the trees peter out and there's a small meadow, the creek running through the middle of it.

I walk around in the meadow a bit, checking it out. The grass is thick and knee-high all around the edges of the meadow. It should be enough to hide the rope.

I walk back up the path in time to meet Timmons and Gimpy coming up with their axes, still arguing about who's better at chopping. I tell them what I'm thinking. They look a little confused.

"You really think that'll work?" Gimpy asks.

"It better," I say.

"The further we can shinny up those trees before we tie the ropes off, the better," Timmons says.

"No one shinnies up trees better than I do," Gimpy says, looking like he's going to run up one right then.

"Stop," I say before Timmons can reply. "Don't say anything unless I tell you to."

We walk around in the trees and pick out two that will work, one on each side of the path.

I go over to the livery and find that the rope is almost ready. When it is, we carry it down to the creek and start laying it out around the perimeter of the meadow, making sure it's well hidden in the grass.

In a few minutes we have the rope into place, the ends running to the two trees that are going to be chopped down. Gimpy and Timmons each take hold of an end and start climbing. When they get up as high as they can go, they tie the ropes to the tree trunks. Timmons makes it back to the ground a few seconds ahead of Gimpy.

"It wasn't fair," Gimpy said. "Not at all. You got a head start. We need to go again."

"Gimpy!" I snap. "What did I say about talking?"

He frowns at me. "Not to?"

"Exactly." I make sure I have both their attention before I continue on. "Cut them part way down, but not the whole way. Get them to where you can drop them with just a couple of chops."

Now there's nothing to do but wait.

50

It's early afternoon when Billy comes back, riding hard. His horse skids to a halt in front of the sheriff's office and he blurts out, "They're coming, Ace! They're coming!"

I look up at the church bell tower and wave to the man sitting up there. He starts ringing the bell.

"How many?" I ask Billy.

"I counted twenty-six of them. They're packing a lot of iron."

Twenty-six. About what we counted on. We head on down to the trap, where the rest of them are waiting. I look the trap over. It looks pretty good for the most part. "I can still see the rope over there. Toss a few more leaves on it," I tell Slow Eye. "Everyone get in position. Stay out of sight and wait for my signal."

I ride on back through town. The place is completely empty. Everyone should be well hidden back in the forest by now, staying low. I ride up to the church and dismount. The bell is quiet, the man who rang it off with the rest of the townsfolk. I whack Coyote on the butt. "Make yourself scarce, horse." He trots off and disappears into the trees.

I climb up into the bell tower. With my looking glass I can see them pretty well. Well enough to see that Wilkins is in the lead.

I watch them for a few minutes, then climb back down. I've got a spot picked out behind the sheriff's office where I can stay hidden in the trees, but still have a good view of the town. I'm wearing my moccasins so that when I need to I can move fast and quiet. Then I hunker down to wait.

About ten minutes pass and I hear them splashing across the creek. A minute later they come into view. They're spread out a bit, rifles out, looking hard for the ambush waiting for them. They stop about fifty yards from town and I hear Wilkins' voice.

I can't hear what he's saying, but when he's done one of his men rides forward alone. He goes most of the way down Lily Creek's only street, looks around, and trots back.

They must like what he tells them because they come on into town, heads swiveling, looking for gun barrels in the windows, on the roofs. I'm glad we didn't go with the roof idea. These are men who've smelled gunpowder a few times. Some are probably war veterans. We'd be able to shoot down a few, but they wouldn't panic under fire and the return fire would be swift and deadly.

"Ain't nobody here," one of them says.

"Looks like they up and left," another adds.

"Don't be too sure of that," Wilkins says, standing up in his stirrups to look into the sheriff's office window. "He's a tricky one. He might have something planned."

"If he's as smart as you say," a man with long yellow hair riding a palomino says, "then maybe he finally realized this fight he can't win. Once he high-tailed it, the rest ran off too."

One of the riders pulls a torch out of his saddlebags. "Can we burn it down now?"

C'mon, Virgil, I whisper to myself. Now's the time.

Like he heard me, Virgil's voice comes floating through the air right then.

"Oh my darling, oh my darling, oh my darrrrling Clementiiiine!"

He's rusty and off-key. It sounds awful, but it does what it's supposed to. It gets their attention.

"Shut up!" Wilkins says. "You hear that?"

"Sounds like someone's killing a cat," yellow-hair says.

"It's coming from over there. Let's go check it out. Stay sharp, boys. Keep your eyes peeled."

The men ride on down the street toward the sound of Virgil's voice. I notice that Wilkins falls back a little so he's in the middle of the pack. If it's a trap, he doesn't plan on being the first one caught in it. It's about what I expected from him.

I parallel them, staying under cover and quiet. They get to the end of the street and pause.

"Sounds like it's coming from down to the crick," one of the men says.

From where they are they can't see Virgil yet. There's too many trees between them and the creek.

195

They head on into the trees and I follow, circling wide and heading for a spot I picked out ahead of time. Since I can cut off through the forest at an angle, I get there about the same time they do and duck behind a tree, then peer around it.

I don't know who's more surprised at what they find down at the creek, them or me. At first I can only stare, surprised. This isn't what we planned. Virgil was supposed to be hunkered down by the creek, making like he was catching frogs.

But he isn't.

Instead he's sitting in the creek with nothing but his coonskin hat on. He's got a little piece of soap and he's lathering up his skinny chest, singing like it's Judgment Day.

The riders approach him and Virgil stops singing and looks up, acting like he only then noticed them.

"What the hell are you doing here, old man?" Wilkins calls out.

Virgil squints at the bar of soap in his hand, then at Wilkins. "What kind of damn fool question is that? Can't you see I'm taking a bath? Hain't you never heard of a bath, sonny?"

That brings a chuckle from a few of the riders and Wilkins' face darkens. He draws his pistol and points it at Virgil.

"You ain't supposed to be here. Why didn't you clear out with the rest?"

"There's no need to point that shootin' iron at me, sonny. I ain't about to cause any problems. I don't live in Lily Creek and I never have. I got me a little cabin up the mountainside. Jes' let me finish my bath and I'll mosey on my way."

Wilkins cocks his pistol. "You'll get on your way right now or you'll get shot."

"All right, all right, I'll git. Don't get your petticoats in a twist."

Virgil stands up. He's buck naked. It's not a pretty sight.

The riders recoil, some of them turning their faces away.

I figure now's the time to spring the trap. Virgil's job was to distract them and I don't think they'll ever be more distracted than they are right now. Those who haven't turned away are staring at the naked old man, water dripping everywhere, skinny as an old rooster, and red from the cold water.

I give a blue jay call. From off in the trees behind the riders comes a few thunks in rapid succession.

Heads turn. "Is that someone chopping wood?" yellow-hair asks.

The trees we chose are big, a hundred feet tall at least, and I can see the tops moving as they start to fall. For a split second nothing seems to happen. A few of the riders are turning their horses. All of them are staring around, wondering what in the world is going on.

Then gravity takes over and the trees pick up a whole lot of speed. Real quick.

The rope, which runs in a big semi-circle clear around that little meadow the riders are clustered in, rises up from where it's hidden in the grass and snaps across the meadow quick as a striking snake.

It hits their horses about chest-high and the horses do what horses always do when something unexpected and scary happens.

They panic.

Those in the front are knocked back into the ones behind them. Half go down in an instant and the other half go into a frenzy. Bucking and squealing, trampling the downed riders underfoot.

I jump to my feet and start firing as fast as I can, followed closely by Lou, Wilson, Billy and Slow Eye. Virgil drops down, snatches up his pistol from where it's hidden in the grass, and charges at the rearing, squealing, shouting mass of men and horses, firing every step of the way.

They never really have a chance. Those whose horses didn't go down are having their hands full trying not to get bucked off. And the thing about riding a bucking horse? It kind of takes all your concentration. There's not much left for shooting your weapon, much less aiming it at anything in particular.

Oh, they still get shots off, but they either shoot each other or into the air. None of the bullets come close to us.

In less than a minute it's over and there's no one shooting back. Most of the gunmen are down and not moving. A few are rolling around on the ground, moaning in pain. A couple riderless horses are running off through the trees.

As I walk up to them, yellow-hair rolls up on his knees and tries to shoot me, but I kick the gun out of his hand before he can bring it to bear. The next kick is under the chin and his head snaps back and he goes limp.

"Woooeeee!" Billy yells, running out into the meadow. "That worked exactly like you said, Ace!"

The others come out of hiding then too, everyone yelling. Virgil is jumping up and down and cackling madly. He's still naked.

"Put some clothes on, before I wish I'd lost my other eye," Lou growls at him.

Virgil suddenly realizes he's not wearing anything and he gets a little redder. He yanks off his coonskin hat and covers himself with it. I wonder how he'd feel if he knew Lou was a woman.

"I wasn't sure that would work," Lou says. "But it sure enough did."

"I never doubted," Billy says. His eyes are glowing and his voice is cracking, like it always does when he gets too excited. "I knew it would work."

I'm glad he was so positive. I had my doubts the whole way.

"What are you going to do about the wounded?" Lou asks. "Can't leave them lying here."

I cut off Virgil before he can speak. "No, you're not shooting them, Virgil."

"You got funny ideas of frontier justice," he grumbles, but then heads off to fetch his clothes. I turn back to Lou.

"Take Wilson with you and go get a couple of wagons. I'll get some bandages. We're going to bind up the ones who are still alive and pile them into one wagon. We'll put the dead in the other and haul them over to the Hashknife. Let them deal with them."

Timmons comes running up then. "One of them got away, Ace."

"Want me to go after him?" Billy asks.

"Let him go. One man can't cause us any trouble."

51

It's sunset, the day after the big battle. The people of Lily Creek have put out a big spread to thank us for what we did. They set out some long tables in the meadow by the church, hung up some lanterns, built a fire. All day a whole hog and a half beef have been slow cooking in a pit barbecue. The tables are fairly groaning under all the food.

We're sitting down, fixing to tuck into all that grub, when Billy looks up and says, "Well, now I seen everything."

"What the hell?" Gimpy cries. "Lou, why you wearing a dress?"

I turn and when I see what they're talking about I almost choke on my tongue.

Walking up with Pearl is Lou, but it isn't the Lou I'm used to. It's like Gimpy said. She's wearing a dress. Not just that, but her hair is fresh cut and it looks like there's rouge on her cheeks. Hell, she isn't even chewing tobacco.

"Quit yer starin'," Lou growls at the gang. "Ain't you never seen a lady before?" It's strange hearing that gruff voice come out of a woman.

"But I'm...but you're..." Slow Eye stammers. "I *peed* in front of you, Lou!"

"Don't worry, I didn't see nothing," she snaps. She turns on Pearl. "I told you this was a bad idea. I'm going and changing into my regular duds."

"C'mon, Lou. You can do this," Pearl says.

"My legs feel cold."

"It's plenty warm."

"Did you know he was a she?" Billy asks me in a low voice. He can't seem to stop staring. I don't think he's even blinked since Lou showed up.

"I did."

"Why didn't you tell me?"

"Because it isn't my business to do so. And it's not yours to know unless she wants to tell."

"Ever' day is full of wonders," Billy says.

Lou takes a seat on the bench next to me.

"The dress looks good on you, Lou."

"Don't make fun of me, Ace. Swear to god I will smack you."

"I'm serious, Lou."

When Lou speaks next her voice is somewhat softer. "Thank you, Ace." She looks around. Most everyone has gone back to what they were doing, which is serious eating. Slow Eye is still staring at her, but Billy kicks him under the table and he looks down at his plate.

"I feel like a damn fool."

"It just takes some getting used to is all."

"I forgot how hard it is being a woman. This dress has hooks and buttons in places I can't reach."

"How long has Pearl known?"

"She said she knew from the first day. Turns out a lot of the women in town figured it out. Just proving what I've always known. Women aren't nearly as blind as men." Lou sounds like the woman I rode the wagon with again, the rough, crusty voice completely gone.

"We see what we want to see," I say.

"I hope you can see what's right in front of your face." Lou gestures with her chin. "Here comes Annie."

Annie walks over, Camila and Diego following her. When they see me they commence to climbing on me and pulling on my coat, yelling my name as if I've forgotten what it is.

"Settle down, children. You know, I saw some watermelon over there. Why don't you two go get yourselves some?"

The children take off and Annie sits down. She looks past me to Lou. "You look lovely, Lou."

Lou smiles and makes a shucks sound. I can't believe what I'm seeing.

"Are you blushing, Lou?"

She elbows me. "It's only the rouge, Ace." She stands up. "I'm going to go get a plate of those ribs."

Under the table, Annie takes hold of my hand and gives it a squeeze. "It's a perfect night, isn't it?"

The moon's coming up, fat and round. Crickets call from the bushes. People are talking and laughing. "Pretty close," I say.

"I can't thank you enough for what you did for us."

"You don't need to."

She slides closer and puts her head on my shoulder. "I could sit here with you forever."

Funny thing is, I'm feeling the same way. It's downright nice, being here with Annie and all these other good folks. It's not something I'm used to.

Soon enough the kids come racing back. Annie goes and gets some food. People eat until they can't eat anymore, then they eat a little more. We're a couple of hours in when someone busts out a guitar. Someone else chimes in on a fiddle and people start clapping.

"Look at that," Annie says, motioning.

Ancil has gotten up from where he was sitting with some other men. He walks over to Pearl, who's sitting at the end of our table, and holds out his hand. Pearl takes it and they start dancing, whirling and spinning around.

"That doesn't look too bad, does it?" Annie asks me.

Suddenly I don't feel so comfortable. "You want me to dance?"

"Now, there's no need to look like a colt facing a bridle for the first time, Ace. It's only dancing."

"But I don't know how to dance."

"I'll show you."

"Go on and dance," Lou says, smiling wickedly. "Don't be such a chicken."

I let Annie pull me up out of my seat. Billy, Slow Eye and Timmons are grinning like fools. I drop a hand to a gun butt. "One word and I'll shoot the lot of you." They all hold up their hands, but they don't stop smiling.

Annie shows me how to do the two-step and I have to admit it's not that bad. It takes a little getting used to, but I can see why people like it. I especially like twirling her, how her dress flares out around her when I do so.

We're at the edge of the party and I twirl Annie yet again, when suddenly everything changes.

There's movement in the darkness behind her. A figure lunges forward and grabs Annie, putting his arm around her throat and a gun to her head.

"Don't move or I'll kill her," he says.

52

It's Wilkins. He presses the gun in hard against her temple.

"Don't come any closer," he says, baring his teeth. "I'll shoot her."

I feel myself get cold inside. Things slow down and become very hard and clear. "Let her go."

"Ain't you supposed to threaten me? Say, let her go or I'll kill you? Something like that?" he sneers.

"You can still walk away," I tell him. "But that won't last much longer."

He jams the gun in harder. I can see he's shaking. She's gone very white. "I'm not going anywhere without the money. I know there's money. Herm told me you were getting a thousand dollars to defend this town. I want that money. Annie here is going to show me where it is and then we're going to ride out of here and you aren't going to follow me. When I'm far enough away, I'll let her go."

Ancil steps forward and holds his hands up. "Just let her go. I promise you we will not follow you or try to stop you. You have my word on—"

"I told you to shut up!" Wilkins yells. He turns the gun on Ancil and pulls the trigger.

Ancil goes down, blood spreading across his chest, and people scream.

My gun fairly leaps into my hands. In the same motion The barrel swings up and I pull the trigger.

The bullet takes Wilkins high up in the shoulder. He screams and loses hold of Annie, falls backward and drops his gun.

Annie spins away. I stalk forward, my pistol pointing at Wilkins' head.

He stares up at me. He's holding his shoulder with one hand, the blood pouring out between his fingers. "Don't...don't kill me," he gasps. "I surrender."

"You had your chance," I reply.

Lou grabs onto my arm. "You don't have to do this, Ace."

I shake her off. Wilkins is saying something, begging, but I can't hear him. I can't hear Lou. There's a roaring in my ears and my vision has narrowed down to Wilkins and the front sight of my gun.

"No!" he yelps, throwing up his hands…

I fire. Once, then twice more quickly. Wilkins slumps over.

The echoes of gunshots fade away and the party is completely silent, everyone frozen, unsure what comes next.

I whistle for Coyote and he comes running. I leap onto his back.

Annie grabs onto my leg. Tears are running down her face. "Don't do this, Ace. Let it end."

"But it won't." On some level a part of my mind tells me that her tears should be affecting me. I should stop this, take her in my arms and make sure she's okay.

But it can't get past the hardness that has settled on me. My heart is made of stone.

"It won't end until Dace Jackson is dead."

I wheel Coyote and Annie loses her hold on me. She reaches up to me but I kick Coyote in the ribs and he gallops out of there.

We run from the light of the party and out into the darkness, a darkness that can't match what's inside me.

I don't have to kick Coyote again. He knows how I feel. He runs with the wind under his feet and the miles fall away.

The cold darkness draws closer around me with every minute. I was a fool to think that the brutality of the world could be faced down by anything less than death. The only safety lies in killing one's enemies until there are none left to kill. Only then can anyone be safe.

It's a mistake I won't make again.

53

I ride into the Hashknife headquarters. The moon is full in the sky and it sheds a sickly light on the destruction of the stampede. Collapsed buildings are indistinct jumbled piles of darkness, freckled with light.

Buford, Dace's foreman, is standing on the front porch of the main house, a lantern hanging on the wall behind him providing light.

He's stripped down to his trousers. His chest is broad and rippled with muscles. His thumbs are hooked into his belt.

"I knew you'd come," he says. He's chewing on a matchstick. His face is in shadow. "It's you and me now. The way it should be."

"Soon it will be just me," I say, coming to a stop and swinging down off Coyote. I draw a pistol.

"I'm unarmed," he says, holding his hands up to show me. "You shoot me now and you're nothing but a damned yellow-belly. You're mighty slick with those guns. Are you going to hide behind them, or are you going to come out and face me like a man?"

My finger tightens on the trigger. I want to kill him so badly I can taste it. But then I holster the gun and start unbuckling my gun belt.

The darkness inside me is savage joy. I'm eager for this. I want to tear him apart with my bare hands.

He rolls his shoulders and spits the matchstick out. He packs a lot of muscle on his big frame. He's six inches taller than me, he easily outweighs me by fifty pounds and judging by the shape of his nose, he's been in a lot of fights.

That's good. I don't want him to go down too easy. I want him to fight.

I'm two steps from the porch when he launches himself at me. I duck the first blow but he's a lot quicker than a man his size should be and the second one catches me in the mouth.

My head snaps back and I taste blood in my mouth.

I smile.

I smile because I don't have to hold back. I can finally let all the darkness out at once.

The smile throws him a little and he frowns. He comes at me in a new flurry of punches. I block the first two, then his right slips past my guard and connects solidly with my ribs. I grunt with the impact. From the sudden pain he might have cracked one.

My smile gets bigger. It's all teeth.

He hesitates and for the first time he looks uncertain.

A new flurry of blows. A couple of them land, including one on my left eye, but I only feel them distantly. They don't seem all that real.

"What's wrong with you?" he hisses. He's breathing hard from the exertion, sweat starting to run down his face. "Why won't you go down? Why don't you fight back?"

I press in and he rains more blows down on me. I don't care. I welcome the pain. His pain, my pain, it's all the same.

But soon it will all be his.

"Say something!" he yells, stepping back. His breath is coming in big gasps now and all his confidence has fled.

I spit out some blood. "My turn," I say.

My first punch comes clear up from my toes, every bit of me behind it. He's slow bringing his hands up and I hit him square in the mouth.

His head snaps back and I feel teeth come loose.

He counterattacks and two of them land, but they have no more effect than flies. They don't even slow me down.

I start hitting him, as fast and as hard as I can. The world goes kind of black for a minute.

When the light returns Buford is on the ground, crumpled up against the porch steps. Blood pours from his mouth. One eye is swollen shut.

He coughs up blood and raises one hand. "No. Stop. I quit."

I kick him to the side and start up the steps. It's Dace that I really want. He's the one behind this all.

As I go past Buford I see a flicker of light from the corner of my eye. He's pulled a knife from somewhere and is slashing at me with it.

I dodge the blow and grab his wrist, bend his arm back, further, further.

The bone snaps and he screams in pain.

His knife is mine now. I slash and blood sprays.

I look down on him as if from far away. It is the only fitting end for one's enemies.

I step over his body. It's time for Dace Jackson. It's time to end this for good.

54

The room is richly furnished, a thick rug on the floor, a whole wall of books, a large stone fireplace, fine leather furniture.

Dace is sitting staring into the cold fireplace. He looks up when I come in and when he moves I see that he is in a metal chair with wheels on it. He turns the chair to face me.

I walk over to him. Blood drips from the knife I hold by my side, landing on the rug. Soon his blood will join it.

"I'm sorry," he says.

That slows me down. The words make no sense at first and I frown.

"I'm sorry. For everything that happened. You have every right to kill me. I won't resist." He looks down at his legs. Even through his trousers it's obvious they are thin and wasted, little more than sticks. "Not that I could do anything anyway. Polio, you see."

I realize that he's holding something to his chest. An ornate picture frame.

He sees my look and holds it out, turning it so I can see the picture. It's a young man posing in front of a house.

"My son. He died two years ago. That's when Buford took over. I knew what he was doing but I…" His voice catches and a tear starts in his eye. "But in my grief I didn't care. I could only think of Jonathan and how I would never see him again."

He swallows hard and brushes at the tears.

"It was Buford who did all this, you see. By the time I came out of my grief it was too late. Most of the hands were Buford's men. He'd taken over and there was nothing I could do. I don't offer that as an excuse. Buford was a mad dog and I should have had him put down long ago. I offer it as an explanation."

He holds his head up and lays the picture flat in his lap.

"I'm ready now. I'm ready to join Jonathan."

All at once feeling rushes back into me. It is as if I have fallen from a great height into my body. I can't breathe. I look down at the blood dripping from my knife and I feel sick.

What have I done?

Scenes race past my eyes, Annie in tears, Ancil falling, the dead faces of Wilkins and Buford.

I lower the knife and leave the room.

When I get back to Lily Creek it is late. The area where the party was is empty except for one person, sitting by a dying fire. It's Lou.

She stands up as I ride up and slide down. Her eyes take in the blood.

"Is it you, Ace? Did you make it back?"

"It's me," I say. "Barely."

"Did you kill Dace?"

I shake my head. "It wasn't Dace behind it. It was Buford. He was running the whole show."

"I can guess what happened to him, can't I?"

I nod. I feel utterly weary.

"Why don't you go down to the creek and get cleaned up. I'll put some coffee on." As I turn away, she says, "It's a clean wound. Ancil's going to make it."

55

The sun comes up and I put down my cup and stand up. Lou and I have been sitting in the sheriff's office all night, drinking coffee. Neither of us said a word the whole time. I needed to think, to sort through what happened and what will come next. Lou left me to it.

"Any idea where you're headed next?" she asks me.

"I don't know. Away."

"Promise me you'll see Annie before you go. That woman doesn't deserve to be run out on."

I was thinking about doing just that, but I know Lou is right. I've done enough. I don't need to make it worse.

"What are you doing next?" I say to Lou. "Back to Lou the mule skinner or…?" I gesture at her dress.

"I don't know," she admits. "Wearing a dress isn't half bad, once you get used to it again. But I liked the freedom of being a man. There's a lot of the world that's closed to women."

She stands up and when I stick out my hand to shake hers she pushes past it suddenly and gives me a hug instead. "Take care of yourself, Ace."

I saddle Coyote. I've left a few things in the boarding house but I don't want to risk running into Pearl. She gets up too early and she knows everything that happens there. None of that stuff is really important.

I ride down to Annie's house. Before I can knock, she opens the door. With a gasp she crosses the space between us and throws her arms around me. She hugs me for a long time and I feel the wetness of her tears through my shirt.

Finally, I push her back. She looks up at me, searching my eyes.

"You're leaving," she says. "Why?"

"I can't be here. It's not safe for you."

"But…you took care of Dace, didn't you? You…" Her words trail off and what I see in her eyes is the thing I've feared the most all along.

Fear.

Of me.

She knows what I'm capable of now. She knows the darkness. And a part of her will always wonder if that darkness could come for her or her children. No matter what I do she will always wonder.

"I didn't kill Dace. But he won't be bothering you again, I promise you that."

"Then why do you have to go?" Fresh tears are starting and each one burns me like a live coal. I touch her hair and something rips loose inside me. Almost, almost I change my mind.

"We both know why," I tell her. "Besides, some of those men I killed, they'll have brothers who will come looking for me. The law will come sniffing around too. Hard to hide that many bodies."

"But we can—"

I cut her off. "No. We can't. This is something I have to do myself." I take a step back. A world slides in between us. "Make sure the boys get the thousand dollars."

She has her arms wrapped tightly around herself. "Will you come back someday?"

"I don't know. I'll try."

I turn and walk to Coyote, get on and ride away without looking back.

It's the hardest thing I've ever done in my life.

The End

Ace's story continues in
Ace Lone Wolf and the Black Pearl Treasure
(turn to the next page to read the first few chapters)

Loved the book?
Hated it?
Meh?

How about going on Amazon and reviewing *The One-Eyed Mule Skinner* now that you've read it? Your comments are very much appreciated!

(Author's note: Although this is a work of fiction, some characters and events are based on fact. There are some historical notes at the end if you're interested.)

Excerpt from *Ace Lone Wolf and the Black Pearl Treasure*

1.

I wake up to the sound of a pistol being cocked near my head.

There's no sound quite like it. I come awake instantly and reach for one of my Colt .44s.

A boot comes down on my wrist, pinning it to the ground.

"It ain't there no more, half-breed," a voice rasps.

I turn my head and blink the sleep out of my eyes. In the early dawn light I can see that the man staring down at me has washed-out blue eyes. They're utterly cold, those eyes, and they're staring down the sights of a Colt Dragoon right at me.

"What do you want?" I ask him.

"Why you, of course."

I see that he isn't alone. There's at least four more men with him, all pointing guns at me. One of them is grinning at me like he just won first prize at the county fair.

I look back at the one standing on my wrist. "Do I know you?"

"You may know *of* me," he says and smiles. He has a gold tooth. His beard is thin and neatly trimmed and he has a heavy ring on one finger. "But I don't believe you *know* me."

I'm starting to get irate. I don't like having a gun shoved in my face and I don't like being called a half-breed, even if it's what I am, what with my mother being a full-blood Chiricahua Apache and my father being a white man. "Get off my damn hand already."

"Don't you talk like that," one of the others says.

He's got a pinched-up face and a narrow chin that disappears into his neck. He's got a mustache but no beard. If I was missing my chin like he is, I'd grow a beard. If I could grow one anyway, which I can't.

"I'll shoot you right here and now. Say I won't."

"Say you won't what?" I ask, not sure what he just said.

"Say I won't do it!" he crows. "Go on, say it!" He's hopping from one foot to another like he's got ants crawling up his legs. I figure he's about two shakes away from shooting me.

"Dial it back, Jesse," the cold-eyed one says.

"You ain't spoiling the fun again like last time!" one of the others blurts out. This one's hat is pushed back so I can see the front of his head has all gone bald. One of his eyes is squinched about halfway shut like maybe a hornet stung him or something. "You always do this, Jesse, go off all half-cocked and start spraying lead everywhere. Not this time, I'm telling you. Not this time!"

"Shut up, Cole," the first one says. "You don't talk to my brother like that or I'll shoot the damned Injun right here and now."

Okay, I don't like the way this whole palaver is going. I might as well speak up, get my say in while I still can.

"Before anyone shoots me, can I find out why?"

"Your horse," the cold-eyed one says. "It's stolen. Though why anyone would steal such an ugly horse is beyond me."

"Watch what you say about Coyote," I say. "That's my horse you're talking about."

I have a deep fondness for that horse. I can't deny that he *is* ugly though, with his jug head and short legs.

"Your stolen horse."

"I paid for that horse, mister," I say.

"If that's so," Jesse says, waving his gun at me. "Then show us the bill of sale."

"What? I don't have a bill of sale. That's crazy talk. I paid for him and he's mine."

"That Rocking R brand on his hip says otherwise," the cold-eyed one says.

"Yeah, we heard they're having real trouble with rustlers and horse thieves and here you show up with one of their horses and no bill of sale," Jesse says. "It don't take a genius to put two and two together."

"And what's two and two make?" I ask him. I know it's stupid to provoke him, but hell, I'm probably going to die anyway. Might as well get in what I can.

"Two and two?" he says, his forehead wrinkling. He puzzles this for a second. "Ain't that just a saying, Frank?" he says, turning to the one with the cold eyes. "Ain't it? How'm I supposed to know what it means?"

214

"I don't cotton much to those who pick on my brother," Frank says, his eyes slitting down.

"So that means what? That you're going to kill me? Aren't you planning on doing that anyway?" I know. I have a problem. I can't keep my mouth shut.

Frank grinds my wrist under his boot. It hurts but I won't give him the satisfaction of showing it.

"What we have here," Frank says to the others, "is a gen-yoo-ine horse thief. And what do we do with horse thieves?"

"We string 'em up!" Cole hoots. He's all kinds of excited. This is the thing he's been waiting for.

"This isn't about stealing a horse, is it?" I ask Frank. He's the only one with enough sense in his head to buy a penny candy.

"Well, sure it is," he says. "What else would it be?"

"Because this is Montana. And the Rocking R is a New Mexico brand. Probably you've never even been there."

"I hear it's warm," Jesse says, shivering a little.

It's a cold morning, winter just past. There's frost on the ground and our breath leaves little clouds in front of our faces.

Suddenly it all makes sense. "You followed me from Virginia City, didn't you?"

"We saw the coin you were spending," Jesse says. "Only one way a half-breed like you gets hold of that kind of scratch and that's by stealin'!"

"Or I got it by spending the winter cowboying on the Double X Ranch. I earned every penny of it." And I did too. Coldest goddamned winter I ever spent in my life. Snow up to my eyebrows. Wind that cut like a knife, coming down from Canada. Feeding hay to cows in the dark and the snow. Rescuing calves with the bad sense to be born in the winter.

When I came up here I just wanted to get far away from everything that could remind me of Annie. Now I just want to get south as fast as I can and get warm.

Except I hadn't counted on getting hung.

"It doesn't matter what I say, does it?" I ask.

Frank gives a little smile and shows that gold tooth again. "No. It don't." He shoves his Dragoon right up to my face. "Bring the rope, Jim. It's time to fix our friend a little going-away party."

Hands grab me and drag me to my feet. My hands are bound behind my back and a noose is dropped over my head.

It's hanging time.

2

"Ain't you caught his horse yet?" Jesse yells.

"Damned critter won't let me get close to it!" a voice yells back. "It keeps running off."

"Use your rope!" Jesse yells back. He grins at me, showing off a pretty impressive snaggle tooth. "We're going to hang you using your own horse. How do you like that?"

"Good luck with that," I tell him.

"Luck ain't got nothing to do with it."

"You're right there."

He scowls at me, trying to figure out if I'm making fun of him.

"You won't catch Coyote unless he wants to be caught," I say. "And I guarantee you he doesn't want to be caught." I hear running hooves and a man cursing off in the trees behind me and smile. Coyote's too smart for these clowns.

"Maybe we'll just shoot the damned horse then," Jesse says.

I fix him with my coldest, dead-eye stare. "You shoot that horse and I promise you I will hunt you down and torture you. When I'm done with you there won't be enough left for the buzzards to eat."

He starts to make a smart comment but a shadow comes over his face and he looks uncertain instead.

Frank backhands me. "Empty words, coming from a dead man."

"I'm Apache," I tell him. "Grandson of the great chief Cochise. You ever fight Apaches before, pale face?" That gets his attention.

"We don't have Apaches in Missouri," Jesse says.

"I heard of Apaches before. They're reckoned to be fierce fighters," Cole says and the man next to him nods in agreement. The man is ugly enough that I reckon he's Cole's brother.

I spit some Apache at them, fast and angry. Jesse, Cole and his brother flinch a little. Only Frank seems unmoved.

"We don't die like ordinary men," I say. "Kill an Apache and he'll crawl out of his grave and gut you in your sleep."

"I don't believe in haunts," Jesse says, but his eyes are wide and there's a quiver in his voice says it's a lie.

"Don't listen to him," Frank says. "He's just trying to rattle you. A man's dead and that's that."

I rattle off some more Apache and bare my teeth at them.

"What's that?" Jesse says. "What'd you just say?"

I smile at him real cold. "It's an Apache death curse." Which it isn't, since there's no such thing, but what do I have to lose? They're already planning to kill me and dead's dead, like Frank said.

"Let's just kill him and get it over with," Cole says. That swole-up eye of his is twitching. "This ain't fun anymore." He points his gun at me. His hand is shaking a little.

"Climb down," Frank hisses. "I say we're hanging him and that means we're hanging him." His voice goes low and deadly. "Unless you're thinking maybe you should be the leader of this gang now, Cole?"

Cole starts shaking his head, babbling how it ain't like that at all. I can't blame him all that much. Frank is clearly a bad hombre. If I live through this, that's something I'm going to remember.

"Bring your horse over here, Bob," Frank says to Cole's brother. "We'll use it."

"He ain't gonna shit on my saddle, is he?" Bob yelps. "I seen plenty of men crap themselves when they hang."

"Really?" Frank says. "How hard is this to figure? He isn't going to be in your saddle anymore once he hangs."

"Oh," Bob says. "That's right." He hustles off to fetch his horse.

Another man shows up then, all out of breath. He's got the same vacant look in his eyes that tells me he's another brother to Cole and Bob. I guess it's true what they say, about good things coming in threes. Or is that bad things? I can never remember.

"I had to give up. The horse run off."

"Forget it, Jim," Frank says. He sounds disgusted.

"That ain't no natural horse," Jim says. "There's something in his eyes. It's like he was reading my mind."

"I said forget it," Frank snaps. He's holding the rope that is tied around my neck and now he tosses the other end up at a pine tree limb overhead.

The throw falls short. So does the next one. It's harder than it looks, tossing a rope over a tree limb.

"Shinny up there and loop this over that limb," Frank snaps at Cole, who puts up his hands and steps back.

"You know I fell out of a tree as a kid, Frank," he protests. "It's how I got this eye like it is."

Frank curses under his breath and turns to Jim. "Since you can't manage to catch one ugly horse, maybe you can do this."

Okay, now I'm mad. No one calls Coyote ugly but me. The fact that he *is* ugly has nothing to do with it.

Jim scoots up the tree, cursing now and then when he scratches himself. He slips the rope over the limb and slides back down. Halfway down he puts his foot on a limb that snaps clean away and he falls the rest of the way, landing with a thud. Jesse giggles.

Bob comes up with his horse. Together they hoist me onto its back. I don't fight them. An idea has been coming to me.

I just might survive this.

Then I'm sitting on his horse. Frank pulls the rope snug and ties off the other end to the tree. I look around at a fine Montana morning, birds coming out, squirrel racing up a nearby tree, snow-capped peaks in the distance. If I'm going to die here, there's worse places.

"Any last words?" Frank says.

"My spirit's coming after you. It won't rest until you're all dead."

Jesse pales and makes the sign of the cross, except he gets it backward. I'm not Catholic and even I know that.

"Goddamn it," Frank says to me in a low voice. "Would you knock that shit off? You already scared him. He's going to be up half the night shivering in his blankets now and I'll have to sit up with him."

I spit some Apache at him.

Frank shakes his head. "In the days to come, when I'm bored or tired, I'm going to think about your body, hanging here from this tree, the crows eating your eyes."

"The crows are smart enough to stay away from the body of an Apache warrior."

Frank shrugs and steps back. "I'm done with you." He looks at the others. "You got all his gear?"

"All loaded up," Cole says.

"Then mount up. We've got places to go and we've wasted enough time with this Injun."

Once they're all mounted up he smiles at me, showing me that gold tooth one more time. "Be seeing you," he says.

He swats the horse on the butt and it jerks forward. Suddenly there's nothing but air underneath my boots.

NOTES ABOUT THE STORY

Although this is a fictional tale, there are elements of historical fact mixed into it.

Ace's character is very, very loosely based on an actual historical figure named Niño Cochise. (And I mean *loosely*. For one thing, Niño was full-blooded Apache.) Niño Cochise was the grandson of the famous Apache chief Cochise. Under the leadership of his mother (Cochise was already dead by then and his father was in Washington, D.C.), Niño's clan slipped away while the Chiricahua Apaches were being transferred to another reservation.

They fled to an old Apache stronghold in the Sierra Madre Mountains in Mexico (which is described more in *The Lost Temple of Totec*). There they lived for several decades, trying to stay hidden from the world as much as possible, forming alliances with American ranchers in the area, Tarahumara Indians, and even with their old enemies, the Yaqui Indians. In the 1900s the stronghold was gradually abandoned as Niño's people moved out into the world.

All of this is detailed in the fascinating autobiography called *The First Hundred Years of Niño Cochise*, told by Niño Cochise to A. Kinney Griffith. I think what I like best about it is that theirs is a story of hope. While most Native Americans were forced onto reservations, they were able to remain free. When they did enter the larger world, they did so on their own terms and by their own choice.

Ike Clanton and Colonel Kosterlitzky were actual historical figures. After the gunfight at the OK Corral, Ike filed murder charges against the Earps. The Earps were acquitted, but Wyatt later pursued a personal vendetta against Ike. Kosterlitzky was the son of a Russian Cossack and a colonel in the Rurales (sort of a Mexican version of the Texas Rangers) for many years. He was truly a larger-than-life character.

Lou is based on a stagecoach driver by the name of Charley Parkhurst, or One-Eyed Charley. Charley was known as one of the finest drivers on the West Coast. But when he died and neighbors came to lay out the body, to their surprise they discovered that he was actually a she. Charlotte ran away from

221

an orphanage at age 12, then adopted a masculine persona. At 21 she went west and spent the rest of her life pretending to be a man.

The Hashknife Ranch was the biggest ranch in Arizona. None of the characters associated with it have any basis in fact. There was no town of Lily Creek. (Which is too bad, because it seems like it would be a nice place to live.)

ABOUT THE AUTHOR

Born in 1965, I grew up on a working cattle ranch in the desert thirty miles from Wickenburg, Arizona, which at that time was exactly the middle of nowhere. Work, cactus and heat were plentiful, forms of recreation were not. The TV got two channels when it wanted to, and only in the evening after someone hand cranked the balky diesel generator to life. All of which meant that my primary form of escape was reading.

At 18 I escaped to Tucson where I attended the University of Arizona. A number of fruitless attempts at productive majors followed, none of which stuck. Discovering I liked writing, I tried journalism two separate times, but had to drop it when I realized that I had no intention of conducting interviews with actual people but preferred simply making them up.

After graduating with a degree in Creative Writing in 1989, I backpacked Europe with a friend and caught the travel bug. With no meaningful job prospects, I hitchhiked around the U.S. for a while then went back to school to learn to be a high school English teacher. I got a teaching job right out of school in the middle of the year. The job lasted exactly one semester, or until I received my summer pay and realized I actually had money to continue backpacking.

The next stop was Australia, where I hoped to spend six months, working wherever I could, then a few months in New Zealand and the South Pacific Islands. However, my plans changed irrevocably when I met a lovely Swiss woman, Claudia, in Alice Springs. Undoubtedly swept away by my lack of a job or real future, she agreed to allow me to follow her back to Switzerland where, a few months later, she gave up her job to continue traveling with me. Over the next couple years we backpacked the U.S., Eastern Europe and Australia/New

Zealand, before marrying and settling in the mountains of Colorado, in a small town called Salida.

In Colorado, after starving for a couple of years, we started our own electronics business, because electronics seemed a logical career choice for someone with a Creative Writing degree.

Around the turn of the century we had a couple of sons, Dylan and Daniel (I say 'we', but when the hard part of having kids came around, there was remarkably little for me to do). Those boys, much to my surprise, have grown up to be amazingly awesome people, doubtless due to their mother's steadying influence during their formative years, and not to the endless stream of bad jokes and puns spewing from their father.

In 2005 we shut the business down and moved back to Tucson. I am currently writing full time.

Made in the USA
San Bernardino, CA
26 January 2019